SHADOWSEER: LONDON

(SHADOWSEER, BOOK ONE)

MORGAN RICE

Morgan Rice

Morgan Rice is the #1 bestselling and USA Today bestselling author of the epic fantasy series THE SORCERER'S RING, comprising seventeen books; of the #1 bestselling series THE VAMPIRE JOURNALS, comprising twelve books; of the #1 bestselling series THE SURVIVAL TRILOGY, a post-apocalyptic thriller comprising three books; of the epic fantasy series KINGS AND SORCERERS, comprising six books; of the epic fantasy series OF CROWNS AND GLORY, comprising eight books; of the epic fantasy series A THRONE FOR SISTERS, comprising eight books; of the new science fiction series THE INVASION CHRONICLES, comprising four books; of the fantasy series OLIVER BLUE AND THE SCHOOL FOR SEERS, comprising four books; of the fantasy series THE WAY OF STEEL, comprising four books; of the fantasy series AGE OF THE SORCERERS, comprising eight books; and if the new fantasy series SHADOWSEER, comprising five books (and counting). Morgan's books are available in audio and print editions, and translations are available in over 25 languages.

Morgan loves to hear from you, so please feel free to visit www.morganricebooks.com to join the email list, receive a free book, receive free giveaways, download the free app, get the latest exclusive news, connect on Facebook and Twitter, and stay in touch!

Select Acclaim for Morgan Rice

"If you thought that there was no reason left for living after the end of THE SORCERER'S RING series, you were wrong. In RISE OF THE DRAGONS Morgan Rice has come up with what promises to be another brilliant series, immersing us in a fantasy of trolls and dragons, of valor, honor, courage, magic and faith in your destiny. Morgan has managed again to produce a strong set of characters that make us cheer for them on every page....Recommended for the permanent library of all readers that love a well-written fantasy."
--*Books and Movie Reviews*
Roberto Mattos

"An action packed fantasy sure to please fans of Morgan Rice's previous novels, along with fans of works such as THE INHERITANCE CYCLE by Christopher Paolini.... Fans of Young Adult Fiction will devour this latest work by Rice and beg for more."
--*The Wanderer, A Literary Journal* (regarding *Rise of the Dragons*)

"A spirited fantasy that weaves elements of mystery and intrigue into its story line. *A Quest of Heroes* is all about the making of courage and about realizing a life purpose that leads to growth, maturity, and excellence....For those seeking meaty fantasy adventures, the protagonists, devices, and action provide a vigorous set of encounters that focus well on Thor's evolution from a dreamy child to a young adult facing impossible odds for survival....Only the beginning of what promises to be an epic young adult series."
--*Midwest Book Review* (D. Donovan, eBook Reviewer)

"THE SORCERER'S RING has all the ingredients for an instant success: plots, counterplots, mystery, valiant knights, and blossoming relationships replete with broken hearts, deception and betrayal. It will keep you entertained for hours, and will satisfy all ages. Recommended for the permanent library of all fantasy readers."
--*Books and Movie Reviews*, Roberto Mattos

"In this action-packed first book in the epic fantasy Sorcerer's Ring series (which is currently 14 books strong), Rice introduces readers to

14-year-old Thorgrin "Thor" McLeod, whose dream is to join the Silver Legion, the elite knights who serve the king…. Rice's writing is solid and the premise intriguing."
   --*Publishers Weekly*

Books by Morgan Rice

SHADOWSEER
SHADOWDEER: LONDON (Book #1)
SHADOWSEER: PARIS (Book #2)
SHADOWSEER: MUNICH (Book #3)
SHADOWSEER: ROME (Book #4)
SHADOWSEER: ATHENS (Book #5)

AGE OF THE SORCERERS
REALM OF DRAGONS (Book #1)
THRONE OF DRAGONS (Book #2)
BORN OF DRAGONS (Book #3)
RING OF DRAGONS (Book #4)
CROWN OF DRAGONS (Book #5)
DUSK OF DRAGONS (Book #6)
SHIELD OF DRAGONS (Book #7)
DREAM OF DRAGONS (Book #8)

OLIVER BLUE AND THE SCHOOL FOR SEERS
THE MAGIC FACTORY (Book #1)
THE ORB OF KANDRA (Book #2)
THE OBSIDIANS (Book #3)
THE SCEPTOR OF FIRE (Book #4)

THE INVASION CHRONICLES
TRANSMISSION (Book #1)
ARRIVAL (Book #2)
ASCENT (Book #3)
RETURN (Book #4)

THE WAY OF STEEL
ONLY THE WORTHY (Book #1)
ONLY THE VALIANT (Book #2)
ONLY THE DESTINED (Book #3)
ONLY THE BOLD (Book #4)

A THRONE FOR SISTERS
A THRONE FOR SISTERS (Book #1)
A COURT FOR THIEVES (Book #2)
A SONG FOR ORPHANS (Book #3)

THE GIFT OF BATTLE (Book #17)

THE SURVIVAL TRILOGY
ARENA ONE: SLAVERSUNNERS (Book #1)
ARENA TWO (Book #2)
ARENA THREE (Book #3)

VAMPIRE, FALLEN
BEFORE DAWN (Book #1)

THE VAMPIRE JOURNALS
TURNED (Book #1)
LOVED (Book #2)
BETRAYED (Book #3)
DESTINED (Book #4)
DESIRED (Book #5)
BETROTHED (Book #6)
VOWED (Book #7)
FOUND (Book #8)
RESURRECTED (Book #9)
CRAVED (Book #10)
FATED (Book #11)
OBSESSED (Book #12)

Want free books?

Subscribe to Morgan Rice's email list and receive 4 free books, 3 free maps, 1 free app, 1 free game, 1 free graphic novel, and exclusive giveaways! To subscribe, visit: www.morganricebooks.com

CHAPTER ONE

Inspector Sebastian Pinsley stood on St George's Field as his hansom carriage left, trying to think of an excuse to avoid going into the building that stood across from him. There were some places that no sane man wanted to set foot in.

Even a little way from the Thames, the stink of it caught his nostrils; although with the city as it was at the moment, it was hard to tell the difference. Barges sat motionless in the distance, though even this early in the morning there were vendors out in the broad square, flanked by buildings. Pinsley observed them as he observed the rest of the world, making sure that he understood what each thing was about before moving on to the next.

He reached into his waistcoat and checked his pocket-watch: five in the morning, far too early to be about. It was certainly too early to be heading into the square-built, high-windowed building that sat before him: Bedlam.

Technically, it was the Bethlem Royal Hospital for the insane, but no one Pinsley knew used that name. It was always Bedlam. It was a name that would conjure fear in anyone, given its history, and Pinsley felt a faint trickle of that fear now. The so-called hospital had once been a byword for the worst of madhouses. They said it had improved since they'd torn down the old building in '15, but still, the mere sight of the place made him shudder. It took Pinsley a moment to realize what it was about the building that threatened him so much: a place like this was the antithesis of the rationality and order he tried to bring to the world. His aunt had ended her days in a place like this. Although it was a small thing compared to some of the losses in his life, the thought of it was still nearly too much.

Inspector Pinsley tightened his dark great coat around the slenderness of his frame, and removed his top hat in preparation to make his entrance. He was unshaven today, so that stubble showed between the spaces of his dark mutton chops, making him seem a little older than his forty-five years. He resolved to return home, or at least to his club, if he could before he made his way to the station. An inspector should set an example for his men.

He strode to the door with the crisp gait that came from military habit, rapped twice upon the knocker, and waited in stillness, the better to hide his nerves at approaching this place. The man who opened the door was portly and dressed in the simple clothes of one of the keepers who would work under the warden. The hallway behind him was dusty with lack of care, wood paneled and stone floored. A portrait of Queen Victoria sat above a desk there, as if its presence would lend the place a grandeur that the rest did not.

"Pinsley," the inspector said. "I take it I am expected?"

"Yes, sir," the man replied. "Please, follow me."

"A moment please," Pinsley said, forestalling the man's march into the building with a raised hand. A wise man gained what information he could before he rushed onto the field of battle, and with an investigation that was doubly true. "Some questions first. There has been no one in or out of the building?"

"Not other than the boy the warden sent to notify you," the keeper said. "It wouldn't be usual in any case. Visitors are in the afternoons."

When they paid a penny for the dubious thrill of staring at the mad. Pinsley bit back his disgust at that and nodded, filing the information away. No visitors meant no likelihood of anyone outside the building. He'd seen the blocky exterior: it was a fortress in all but name.

"The deceased is…"

"A young woman by the name of Greene, sir," the keeper said. "Please, we can't have the doors open too long, even with them all confined to their rooms. Security is important here."

In his head, Inspector Pinsley stopped the silent count that had been going on since their conversation began, trying to judge if the man had left the door open for so long because it was an inspector calling, or simply because he was lax in his duties. A careful study of the man's face and hands revealed them to be surprisingly clean, while his hair was well trimmed, and his work clothes had only the normal level of dirt. A man who took that level of care in those details was likely to be careful in other things, too, so possibly it was just Pinsley's presence that had made him lax about the door.

"We have a visitors' book, sir," the keeper said. "In fact, you should sign it. The warden is quite strict about that. No one in or out without signing to show that they've been."

"Trying to avoid another parliamentary enquiry?" Pinsley said. It was possibly a little sharp, but at this time of the morning, it was hard not to be sharp. It wasn't as if Pinsley slept well, in any case.

The keeper winced at that. "I wouldn't know, sir. You have to sign."

Pinsley stepped into the place, and the cold of it was somehow even greater than it had been outside, in spite of it being February. It was darker than he would have liked inside the asylum, the windows not providing enough light to truly illuminate the place and the gas lights not lit since it was nominally morning. There were shouts and cries in the distance, off down half a dozen corridors. Only one stood quiet.

The keeper gestured to a visitors' book bound in leather. Pinsley opened it to the current day, the 2nd of February, and took a moment to scan through the names there before he signed his own. There had been few enough visitors the day before, all in the afternoon, and none scheduled to visit the deceased, according to the notes on the purpose of their visit. For his own, he wrote simply "the investigation of a death" and left it at that.

"This way, Inspector," the keeper said, gesturing to the quiet corridor. Pinsley didn't wait for him, but marched ahead through the building. It didn't matter that this place frightened him; a man faced his fears of the unknown, and shone the light of reason into the dark.

"Sir, wait for me," the man said, but by the time he caught up, Pinsley had reached an iron gate set into one of the hallways. He tried it, and found it locked. The keeper fumbled for his keys and unlocked it for him with speed.

"This gate is normally kept locked?" Pinsley said.

"Yes, sir."

Pinsley believed him. The keeper had handled the keys with a speed that said he did it as routine, every time he passed. He locked the gate behind them with as much speed. The space beyond had a series of rooms leading off it, each presumably housing an occupant, each fastened tightly as Pinsley checked them.

There were portal windows at eye level on some of the rooms, the way there might have been for prisoners in a more ordinary jail. Pinsley paused at one, then another, forcing himself to look. The figures on this wing were all women. The first Pinsley looked in on was curled up on a cot. The second was back against one of the walls, banging her head slowly against it. The third… Pinsley had to resist the urge to leap back as he found pale eyes staring straight at him.

Fear rose in him, not sudden, not something to be fought the way it had been back in the days before he'd been a police inspector, back in the Crimea. Not the way it had been when he'd seen his beloved

3

Catherine lying dead at the hands of a madman, either. This fear was an older thing, built on memories from his childhood. In that instant, it wasn't Inspector Pinsley walking along the corridor, but young Sebastian. How old had he been when he'd last seen his aunt, when she'd been sitting by herself, singing one nursery rhyme over, and over, and…

No, he wouldn't think of that. He was a rational man, a man who worked with the mind. To save himself from being buried in memories, he focused on the present, using what he could see of the women he passed to guess at their former lives: governess, seamstress, wife. Everything, from the way someone stood to the callouses on their hands, had a story to tell, and if Pinsley concentrated on it enough, he didn't have to think about the past.

Even doing that, the walk seemed to take forever. Each step was an effort, seeming to echo around the building. It took Pinsley a moment to file away the silence as a piece of a puzzle, because nowhere else in this place was quiet. If Pinsley had been a less rational man, he would have thought that something was holding the people here to silence. Instead, he reminded himself that it was just death, and the fear of it, that was producing such an effect.

Pinsley was only too grateful when they finally reached the room they sought. It was the only one with the door open, and the warden of the building was waiting.

"Warden Buckle, this is Inspector Pinsley," the keeper said.

"An inspector?" the warden said, sounding a little surprised. "He isn't dressed as one."

He was a somewhat shorter man than Pinsley, balding and dressed in a formal frock coat and waistcoat buttoned with large brass buttons. His cravat was rather looser than Pinsley's own scarf, but Pinsley could understand that concession to comfort, given the scene within. It was enough that Pinsley had to take a gasping breath to be able to stomach it.

The room was a relatively simple, white-walled place, forming a square perhaps ten feet on a side. There were two beds within it, covered in grey blankets, and a wash stand to one side. All of it had blood on it. Pinsley had seen worse than this in the war, but that was no consolation now. He had to remind himself that he was there to observe, to understand, and the best way to do that was to shut sympathy away so that he could look this over coldly.

The body of a woman lay on the floor, partially covered by a sheet, which had done nothing to stop the flow of blood. Her hair and face were matted with it, until it was hard to make out many of the details. Pinsley didn't want to look, because for a moment, all he could see was Catherine lying there... no. He would not think of that, not now.

Even so, it was several seconds before he could make himself look at the details of the dead woman's appearance. Her clothes were expensive, or had been once, perhaps a season or two ago. Her hands bore the signs of a struggle, and there were parallel cuts on her arms.

Another woman crouched, huddled in the corner, her hands over her face as if they might block out the scene. There was blood on her hands, in her hair, on the walls around her. She had a bruise swelling around her left eye. She was dark haired and simply dressed, wringing a bonnet between her hands like a rag. She seemed to shake with every step anyone took around her, and was muttering something to herself under her breath.

"The shadows... the shadows..."

"As you can see, Inspector," Warden Buckle said. "It is a relatively simple matter. Elsie here got hold of a knife and decided to strike out at her roommate..."

"Tabitha Greene," the keeper supplied. The warden gave him a look that told Pinsley everything he needed to know about the way the man ran things here. He'd seen men like this in Crimea, determined not to be corrected by a subordinate, whatever the cost.

"As I say," the warden said. "It is a simple matter. Hardly worth troubling you with, given that the only place Elsie might end up for this is... well, *here*."

He made it sound as if murders were common there. Perhaps they were; Pinsley resolved to check, because such a thing could not be allowed to stand.

"Still, I have some questions," he said. "Was the knife found?"

Warden Buckle looked a little uncomfortable at that. "Well... no."

"You checked thoroughly?" Pinsley said. "It is not in one of the other cells?"

"There would be no way to get it there, sir," the keeper said.

"Check anyway, please," Inspector Pinsley said. He took a moment to check the body. He had seen the cuts a knife could cause, and a sword, and a dozen other weapons. These looked like none of those, because they were strangely parallel, the way wounds from claws might have been.

Inspector Pinsley frowned at that. He didn't have enough information yet to make sense of it, and that troubled him. Not understanding might be the first step along the path to reason, but it could also lead to dangerous, intolerable unreason. Especially here.

He went to the young woman who had been left crouching in the corner. "And why was this young woman left here with the body?"

"There was nowhere else to put her," Warden Buckle said. "Besides, it seems right that she is made to confront what she's done. If she weren't *here*, she'd hang for this."

She still might; that would be a matter for a judge. Typically, the law demanded a life for a life. Looking at this young woman, Pinsley wasn't sure he could be sanguine about the harshness of that. Pinsley crouched beside her.

"The shadows…" she whispered.

"Look at me, please."

The young woman didn't do it at first, but Pinsley peeled her hands away from her face.

"I don't want to look!" she cried out. "I don't want to look at it!"

"You don't want to look at what you did?" Pinsley asked.

"I didn't do this!" she wailed. "I didn't. Damn you for saying it. Damn you!"

Warden Buckle took a step towards her as if he might strike her. Pinsley stopped him with a look.

"A blow is a well-known way to stop hysterics," Buckle insisted.

"A blow such as the one you have already struck her?" Pinsley asked. "Don't think I didn't notice the reddening around your knuckles, sir."

"I… how dare you?" the warden asked.

Pinsley ignored him, returning his attention to the young woman. "It's Elsie, isn't it?"

She nodded in between choking sobs.

"Can you tell me what happened here?"

"Any fool can tell you that!" the warden asked.

"I didn't do it!" Elsie repeated. "I didn't. I didn't! It was… there were shadows, strange shadows, and… and… no, I didn't do it!"

"Inspector," the warden said. "I think that is quite enough. The girl is clearly deranged. She was found inside a locked room along with the body. Everything here was locked up tight overnight. There is no way it could have been anyone else."

Pinsley knew that had to be true. He was a man of logic, of science. The man of intellect applied reason until only one answer remained, and here, that answer seemed obvious.

It was just… why was the knife not there?

Why did the cuts on the body look far more like the claws of some wild beast?

Why did he find himself believing this girl when she told him that she hadn't done it?

And what did she mean when she talked about the shadows being strange?

CHAPTER TWO

Kaia weighed the sheets she held, trying not to be too obvious about it, looking past the other girls in the dormitory as she considered her plan. The windows of the Sydney Street Foundling Hospital were set high, out of the reach of the children within. In theory, it was to prevent distractions, but everyone there knew that it was to make it harder for those within to simply escape.

Around her, the other girls were running around, and in moments like this it was almost possible to believe that this was a normal place. The youngest of them were playing a game of pick up sticks in the corner, while a couple of the others were reciting rhymes. It was only the fact that they were doing it quietly, so that Mrs. Garrow wouldn't hear, that reminded her of what this place was *really* like. She said that children should be seen, not heard, and enforced it with all the violence her cane could bring.

Kaia hated that cane. She hated the way the Garrows acted, like they were doing the girls a favor with every punishment. She hated all of it.

She was still thinking about how much she hated the place when the clang of the breakfast bell came from below. The other girls scrambled to put away the few toys they had, lining up in their plain, basic clothes, grey with age and scrubbing. The ones who hadn't made their beds yet did it now, and the older ones checked that the younger ones had washed behind their ears, and all the other places the Garrows might look.

They filed out, and just by not going with them, Kaia was committed to this. There would be a punishment for not doing as the others did. One of the smallest ones glanced back, and Kaia put a finger to her lips. Kaia was determined, because the alternative to running was far, far worse. Tomorrow was her birthday; seventeen, and everyone knew what that meant.

No time to think about that. She had to be brave about this. She had to act.

Kaia started counting under her breath. She had three minutes. Three minutes before Mrs. Garrow came to check on the room, and make notes on which girls deserved her wrath. Three minutes before she found Kaia here, trying to leave.

Using her bed as a platform to climb from, she hauled herself up to the window. Kaia was grateful that her skirts weren't the full hooped ones that most women she saw outside seemed to wear, but the combination of them and layers of underclothes was still enough to slow her climb a little.

She was small for her age, because it wasn't as if the orphanage wanted to spend any more than it had to on food. Every penny Mrs. Garrow and her husband saved meant there was more money in their pocket. At least now, her size allowed her to fit on the small space of the windowsill long enough to slide the window open and fasten a rope made from bedsheets into place. Strands of blonde hair fell around Kaia's heart-shaped face as she looked down. It was a long way down to the street. If she fell...

The answer, Kaia reminded herself, was not to fall. Being scared had never helped her avoid a single punishment. She had to get away.

In theory, tomorrow, Kaia would be able to simply walk out the front door of the place. Girls of seventeen were too old for London's orphanages, by law. Kaia knew it didn't work like that, though. If she did it that way, it would be the workhouse at best, and Mrs. Garrow had already talked about the patron she'd found who was willing to offer a girl like Kaia a position as a servant. Kaia wasn't naive enough to believe that any well-off man did something like that out of the goodness of his heart. She knew she was one of the prettier girls there, and what such a man would want from her in return for the position. She'd stood by her bed with the others when they'd come round, ostensibly touring the building, but also making their choices. If she went, she would be nothing more than a plaything, until her new patron tired of her and threw her out onto the streets. The thought of it disgusted her.

No, she couldn't wait until tomorrow. Dropping down on the sheet, she put her weight against it, hanging there with shoes not really designed for the purpose of scraping against the wall. Kaia had put knots in the sheet, but still, it was a hard climb down to the ground, and a cold one. The first rays of the morning sun were only barely cutting through a mist that threatened to freeze Kaia to the bone, turning that mist red in the dawn.

9

She was close to the ground when her hands slipped from the makeshift rope. Kaia had a moment of pure terror as she fell, but she felt her feet touch the ground after just an instant. She'd fallen a few feet at most. Relief flooded through Kaia, and not just because she'd survived the fall. She was out of the orphanage; she was free. The joy that came from that was tempered only by the need to get away. Kaia paused for only the briefest moment to take in the square, whitewashed exterior of the place that had been her home as long as she could remember. She'd only ever been out of it with the other girls, and now she was free of it. This would, she swore, be the last time she looked on it.

Kaia set off at a run, heading north. She needed to put as much distance between her and the orphanage as possible. The barrow boys were wheeling barrows to market in Covent Garden or Whitechapel. The ones who had early shifts at a factory were making their way out to them from the tenements they shared with a dozen other families.

The filth of the streets was impossible to avoid, and the air was as thick with grime as with fog. They said that you could tell how long a sheep had been in the city by how grey its coat was, and right then, Kaia could believe it. The few horses she saw so early didn't even bother with boys following them to collect their manure. She simply had to pick her way between it all.

Kaia walked quickly, reasoning that the more she lost herself, the harder she would be to find in an hour or two from now when the Garrows noticed that she was missing. Kaia wondered how much effort they would put into looking for her. Another day and she was free to do as she wished, but at the same time, if they'd already taken money from her would-be "benefactor," they might look harder. Better to keep moving.

Kaia had already formed a plan: she would try to reach a station, Paddington or Euston. From there, she could try to slip onto a train heading somewhere, anywhere. Brighton, Liverpool, maybe even go as far north as Scotland. No one would ever look for her there. Even the Garrows wouldn't hunt for her as far as Edinburgh.

The thought of the station kept her moving. If she kept walking north, she would reach it. She would wait outside it all night if she had to. Then it was a question of finding a way onto a railway carriage without being seen, or finding a way to get a ticket to somewhere else. Kaia could do this; she had to tell herself that. She could.

Kaia found herself crossing a bridge, lit by gas lamps at intervals that had yet to be doused for the morning. Even in the fog she thought it was probably Westminster Bridge, with arch after arch reaching down slightly unsteadily into the water. She crossed over into the district, making out buildings in the hazy distance. The Houses of Parliament were bright even this early, and Kaia stared at them in wonderment. Kaia had heard somewhere that their precincts had hundreds of rooms, and that there were servants and cooks on hand to supply anything the members there wanted. Kaia couldn't even imagine living in that kind of luxury. She stared at the buildings now, so close to the place she'd been brought up and so utterly different, all at once.

People walked the other way, heading to what she assumed were offices there in the city. The men who passed, and they were almost all men, were dressed with a wealth that made Kaia feel small and grubby by comparison.

She saw one or two eyes on her as she walked, and flinched at it, thinking that they might see her for who she was and drag her back to Mrs. Garrow. She had to force herself to keep walking, telling herself that she was simply out without a bonnet or a coat. They didn't *know*, however much the fear inside her might tell her otherwise. She might not look like she lived here, but at least, she guessed, she could pass for someone's servant.

How long did she walk for? Long enough that she could feel the chill of the fog in her bones, at least. Long enough that the mist off the river started to clear a little, so that she could make out the shine of the moon above. Long enough that she became hungry, and started to look round for something to eat.

That was the next problem: Kaia had no money, because aside from sixpence at Christmas, the Garrows didn't believe in that kind of generosity towards their wards. She found herself envying the men who passed. Some would be leaving wives who had made them breakfast, or houses with paid cooks. Some would be making their way to their clubs, to settle down in soft armchairs and have food brought.

Kaia *wished* that she could have a life like that. Not even a life like that; she wished that she could just have a life that was safe. In spite of having no way to buy anything, when Kaia scented roasting food on the wind, she found herself drawn inexorably towards a small side street that seemed packed from end to end with food vendors. Kaia waited at the end of it, staring at the sausages and roast chestnuts, eel pies and apples with the longing that came from having walked too far with too little to eat.

What could she do, though? She couldn't just snatch something from one of them. She didn't want to be a thief.

"Out of the way, girl," a big, burly man ordered her, striding along with a cane in one hand that he swung in time with every meaty step. He looked as if he hadn't missed a meal in his life, and would probably trample over anyone who suggested it. He bought so much food from one vendor that Kaia could barely believe it, pies and apples that made Kaia's stomach rumble. He shoved past her again on the way out of the alley, making his way over to a small park, where he sat down by one of the trees, eating with such speed that Kaia thought he might choke with it. He laid out the food he had, while reading from what appeared to be the day's broadsheet.

Kaia drifted closer, thinking that she might be able to beg some small measure of food from him. A man like that, who had so much, and was so rude about it, might not miss *one* apple.

She edged forward, working up the courage to ask. She made her way slowly towards the tree the man was sitting under, trying to convince herself that this stranger might help her. Kaia's nerves at doing it made her almost creep forward towards him.

She found herself staring at the man looking back at her.

"Thief!" He surged to his feet. "Thief, I say!"

"I'm not-"

The man struck out at her before Kaia could begin to explain, lashing out with his cane so that she had to leap back from it. Kaia's terror propelled her away from him, and in a second, she had set off running before she even knew what she was doing. She ran blindly past the trees, towards the wrought iron railings at the far end of the park, not looking back, not slowing down. If she just ran, she could-

A hand clamped onto Kaia's arm, jerking her to a halt, and turning her to face a man dressed in the uniform of a constable. Kaia cried out and tried to break free, but he held onto her, then fastened cuffs onto her wrists.

"Got you!" he said. "Filthy little thief. What are you even doing this end of the city?"

"I… I'm sorry," Kaia said, not understanding. "I'm not a thief. I didn't know I shouldn't be here. I'm sorry."

"Tell that to the beak, girl," the constable said. "Thieving from rich folk? You'll be lucky if you don't find yourself transported off to the colonies."

Horror filled Kaia at those words. The colonies, Australia, meant the other side of the Empire, the other side of the *world*. She'd heard the stories of how brutal things were over there, with the heat, the cruelty of people who ran things. To be sent there was as good as a death sentence.

"But I'm not a thief!"

CHAPTER THREE

The sun was creeping out from the fog when Inspector Pinsley reached St. Bartholomew's hospital for the autopsy of Tabitha Greene.

Pinsley stepped down into Smithfields and took a moment to brace himself against the cold of the February air in the district.

"Get'cher papers!" a crier on one of the corners called. "Government denies involvement in Orsini plot! Victories in the Raj and in China!"

Pinsley ignored him. This wasn't the breakfast table, to be reading the broadsheets. Instead, he stared up at St. Bart's. The building towered above him, three stories tall and fifteen bays wide, dominating one entire end of the square he stood in. It was a building that promised the finest teaching the Empire had in medicine. Pinsley just hoped that it had other answers for him.

A porter eyed him as he stepped inside, probably surprised by the earliness of the visit. He looked presentable enough, at least. He'd had time enough to head back to his club, have breakfast, and shave, but no more than that. He could have headed home, but home held too many memories of Catherine and Olivia. He only kept the place at all because of the possibility that his and Catherine's daughter might come back.

He couldn't concentrate on the past now, though, not when the present held its own troubles. He knew the way to the surgical theatres by now, and strode to them with the stiff backed quickness of a soldier on the march. A few young men were in already, moving from one side of the hospital to the other as they prepared for the morning's work. Automatically, Pinsley picked out one who had been drinking heavily the night before, one who had been in a fight, one whose poorly repaired clothes suggested money troubles he was trying to hide.

He kept going, into the heart of the place, until he came to the surgical theatre he wanted, with a plaque that marked it as the domain of Dr. Jonah Florian. Pinsley took a breath before he stepped inside, steeling himself for what was to come. As he entered, the cold air of open windows hit him so that it was no better than being outside.

14

The room was truly a theater, with circles of benches arranged so that a smattering of students might look down from all sides on the events taking place at the center of the room. A sturdy table stood there, long stained by the procedures that had taken place on it. The body of Tabitha Greene lay on that table, stretched out in that too-still way that only the dead had. Pinsley felt a pang of disquiet at seeing her laid there, as if she were no more than an object of study.

Dr. Florian stood beside her, stripped to shirt sleeves and waistcoat, with a leather apron over the top that might have suited a butcher as much as a surgeon. It didn't help that Dr. Florian *looked* like most people's image of a butcher, thick set and square-featured, sporting a thick moustache and a shaven head, with a ruddiness to his complexion that seemed like the only warmth in the otherwise frigid room. He looked up as Pinsley approached down the steps towards the middle of the room.

"Ah, Inspector," Dr. Florian said with a faint smile. "Here to arrest me as a resurrectionist? I assure you that all bodies here have been procured legitimately, under the Act."

"I know," Pinsley said, ignoring the reference to grave robbery. That hadn't been a problem in London for a decade or more. "I made sure that this body came to you specifically. I would value your opinion."

He heard Dr. Florian sigh. "Of course you would. Is this to be a full inquest? Are we to have a dozen jurors walk in to watch, and a coroner? It seems a little early for them, and I was planning to be away in an hour. I have two amputations to perform, and the possibility of a baby to deliver."

Probably all while wearing the same bloodstained apron.

"Have you read Dr. Semmelweis's thoughts on the effects of washing your hands and your equipment?" Pinsley asked, as casually as he could. It was better not to confront the man too openly when he needed his help.

Dr. Florian laughed at that. "Do I tell you how to investigate a crime, Inspector? The windows are open to prevent miasma, and this patient... well, I doubt that she will get much sicker. Perhaps you feel that I should administer ether before I begin?"

Pinsley gave up. He was here for a purpose, and it wasn't to debate medical procedures.

"What can you tell me about this young woman?" he asked. "She was killed in the early hours of this morning."

15

"Yes," Dr. Florian said. "That is consistent with the level of rigor in the corpse." He started to talk to the wider room. "Note that the body relaxes completely upon death, and that it progressively stiffens, until such time as putrefaction begins. By understanding the process, one can judge the time with relative precision."

Pinsley wanted to hurry the other man along, hated wasting time when there were answers to be found, but knew from experience that Dr. Florian would always proceed at his own pace.

"What else?" he asked.

"Shall we proceed to the cause of death?" the physician suggested. He started to cut away enough of Tabitha Greene's dress to display the claw marks clearly for his students. "Note the parallel gouges, consistent with the claws of some large beast."

Pinsley felt a brief thrill of excitement at that. He'd known that this wasn't down to a simple knife. Then he felt a moment of guilt at that excitement. A woman lay dead.

"Can you guess what kind?" Pinsley asked.

Dr. Florian bestowed an affronted look on him. "I do not *guess,* Inspector. I am a man of science. Suffice it to say that this was not caused by some domestic cat or dog. The claw marks *here* are the key ones. See the way they dissect the carotid artery and the trachea?"

Pinsley nodded. Around him, He could see some of the medical students flinching or struggling to maintain an impassive expression. Pinsley felt as much as they did, but he hid it better now. After all he'd seen in the Crimea, violent death was anything but a stranger. He'd seen men torn open by sword blows and cannon shots, seen others lose fingers to the cold, seen his wife...

...no, he wouldn't think about that. A flash of raw grief shot through him, and Pinsley had to fight to keep it at bay.

"Are you quite all right, Inspector?" Dr. Florian asked.

"Perfectly well, thank you," Pinsley lied. He did his best to ignore the superior looks coming from some of the students. To try to regain control of the situation, he looked closer at the corpse. "Am I right in thinking that the angle of the blows would have been downwards?"

That seemed to catch Dr. Florian a little by surprise. "Yes, I suppose they would have been."

"So a large animal indeed, unless it knocked her to the ground first."

"Yes, I imagine so," Dr. Florian said.

16

Except that an animal that large would have been noted, running around London in the dead of night. It was perhaps plausible that some creature might have escaped the confines of the zoological society's captivity, but for it to then manage to find its way into the middle of Bedlam and out again... no, that made no sense.

The important thing, as far as Pinsley could see, was that Tabitha Greene's cellmate had been somewhat shorter than the woman now lying on the table. It seemed just as improbable that she might have delivered these blows as that a wild animal might have gotten into the room.

"I should also say," Dr. Florian said, "that I have seen frenzied knife attacks that have also inflicted as many wounds on their victims."

"With such strange, parallel cuts?" Pinsley insisted.

"Well... no," Dr. Florian said.

"What else can you tell me?" Pinsley asked the surgeon. He paced around the table, examining the body as if he were the doctor and not the other man.

"What would you have me say?" Dr. Florian countered. "I have established that she died, and from what wounds."

"Are there any signs of a struggle upon her?" Pinsley asked.

"Aside from the cuts?" the surgeon shot back in a weary tone. He looked over the body again. "Her fingernails are ragged, and appear bloody. It seems that she may have fought back against her attacker. Unless you have some trick to link that to a killer, it hardly matters, though."

"It matters in that one young woman who currently stands accused of this has no marks upon her from those nails," Pinsley said, more to himself than to Dr. Florian. "There are cuts on her arms, too. She tried to defend herself against the blows, which meant that she saw her attacker."

Again, though, that didn't seem as if it could link to a particular killer with any certainty. Unless he was about to start placing faith in spiritualists, it wasn't as if he could ask Tabitha Greene who she had seen.

That seemed to be all of it, except... something caught his eye, which had previously been hidden by the neckline of Tabitha Greene's dress. There was a mark on her skin that seemed in almost the shape of an eye, an oval with a central dot and lines above that might have been stylized lashes. Pinsley moved to examine it. The mark was deep and vivid, a deep black that stood out against the paleness of her skin. The

17

edges were defined, but it did not seem to be something on the skin; rather it was a part of the skin itself.

"What is this? A tattoo, a brand, a burn?"

Dr. Florian moved close to examine the mark. "None of those. There is not the scarring one might associate with a burn mark, and it is clearly not the work of needle and ink. No, I would say that this is a birthmark, nothing more."

"A very unusual shape for a birthmark," Pinsley said.

"Perhaps, but I hardly think it will lead you to your killer, do you?"

"No, I suppose not," Pinsley said, trying not to let too much disappointment into his voice. "Still, it is unusual. Could you make a record of it?"

"I can do better than that," Dr. Florian said. He took out a surgical knife. "It will be an opportunity to teach my students the principles of preserving flesh chemically. Now, if that will be all, I still have the principles of anatomical dissection to teach my students using the cadaver's internal organs. Unless you wish to stay and watch."

Pinsley didn't. He wanted nothing more than to be gone from the room at that point. Tabitha Greene might be dead, but even so, this seemed callous. "It may be necessary to have you testify before a coroner, or a court when I catch who did this."

"Of course," Dr. Florian said, with the bad grace of someone who knew that he didn't actually have a choice in the matter. He picked up a surgical knife. "Now, where was I..."

Pinsley left the theater as swiftly as dignity allowed. He couldn't stop Dr. Florian's efforts, when the 1832 Act to stop grave robbery explicitly allowed the use of corpses from poor houses and mad houses for such things. That didn't mean that he had to be there to watch, though.

He headed back out into the open air, gulping in... well, the air of London hardly ever counted as *fresh,* even in winter. Still, it was enough to settle his nerves. He considered flagging down a cab to take him back to the station, but decided to walk instead. He needed time to think.

Somehow, though, Pinsley suspected that no amount of thinking would unpick this tangle. He had evidence pointing to a creature where none could have been, a murder in a locked room with no weapon, and a suspect whose protestations of innocence seemed all too genuine and who was too short to have inflicted the wounds that killed Tabitha

Greene. It all fit together like jarring fragments of clockwork, each grinding against the others in Pinsley's mind, increasing his frustration.

There wasn't even an obvious route to find more evidence. The victim had no visitors to speak to who might know something, and there was no obvious motive for this. Worse, the warden of Bedlam had been adamant that Tabitha Greene's cellmate had done this. That was the kind of accusation that could quickly harden into a certainty, and then become a noose around the young woman's neck. Pinsley had to find an answer before that. He had to.

CHAPTER FOUR

Fear made Kaia wrench at the handcuffs that held her, even though it only made them chafe at her wrists. It certainly didn't let her loose, and it didn't let her break free of the policeman's grip, either. It was cold enough too that she wasn't sure if she was shivering with the fear or with that.

The constable dragged her along, through a large, arched doorway into the lobby of Great Scotland Yard in Whitehall. It was a huge, clean, open space, with a set of tables for officers to attend to business, a large staircase leading up, and solid looking doors leading into the rest of the place. Fear all but consumed Kaia. She'd been in trouble before in the orphanage, because it was impossible to live up to the standards to avoid a thrashing from Mrs. Garrow's cane there. This was different, though, and terrifying. She hadn't even done anything.

"Stop struggling, or I'll clip you round the ear, girl," the bobby who'd arrested her snapped. He dragged her over to a broad table, where a broad shouldered sergeant was keeping notes of those brought in, his blue top hat resting beside a ledger, his long blue overcoat resting on a chair.

"Who's this then?" the sergeant asked, in the tone of someone who felt it was still too early in the morning to care.

"Some little thief," the constable said.

"I didn't steal anything!" Kaia complained. A brief flare of hope rose in her at that, even if it was adrift in a wider wash of fear. This was all happening too fast. She didn't know what was going on, not really. The law was a terrifying thing that had been mentioned in the orphanage only as a source of terror, a threat to level at those who misbehaved.

But she hadn't actually stolen anything. Surely the police would see that? They would see that she didn't have anything stolen on her, that she hadn't been doing anything wrong, and they would let her go. They had to.

"Think anyone will believe that?" the constable demanded, shoving her another step forward towards the desk. "Are you going to tell me that the fine gentleman who accused you was lying? And if you're so innocent, why did you run?"

Kaia felt the hope inside her snuffed out like a candle.

"There will be time enough for all that in front of the magistrate," the sergeant said. He dipped a steel nibbed pen in ink and poised it above the weighty looking ledger. "For now, I want your name, girl."

"Kaia."

"What is that? Irish?" the sergeant demanded.

"I don't know," Kaia said. She yelped as the constable struck the back of her head with the flat of her hand.

"Speak respectfully to the sergeant!" the policeman snapped.

"I don't know, sir," Kaia said, gritting her teeth. She tried to tell herself that it was no worse than having to address Mr. and Mrs. Garrow formally at all times, but it was. The worst the Garrows could do was hit her, or send her away to a position with some rich man that came with expectations she really didn't want. The constable, though... he'd talked about sending her to *Australia*.

Kaia didn't know much about the different parts of the world, since the Garrows hadn't felt it necessary to teach geography, beyond a vague awareness of those parts of the map that fell under the British Empire. Even so, she knew enough about Australia to know that being sent there was almost a death sentence.

"Well, let's try something you do know," the sergeant said. "Like your surname."

"I don't know that either... sir," Kaia said. It earned her another clip around the back of the head.

"Don't lie," the constable said.

"I'm not lying," Kaia replied. She hadn't thought that she could hate anyone else as much as the Garrows, but she was starting to.

"You're trying to tell us that you don't know your surname?" the sergeant said. "What about where you're from? You'd better start explaining, or it will go badly for you. Being uncooperative won't help you with the magistrate."

"Not much will," the constable put in. "Old Colson's on today. As much of a hanging judge as there ever was. You'll be lucky if it's just the colonies for you."

Kaia tried to take a step back at that, wanting to get away from all this, but the constable held her in place. She knew that she *could* explain who she was, but that wouldn't do much to help her now. The best case scenario would be to be sent back to the orphanage, and today was the day she was due to be sold off in all but name. The fear of it kept her caught in silence.

She heard the sergeant sigh again. "I suppose it doesn't make a difference. Where did you find her, Constable?"

"Just hopping the fence of the Victoria Tower Gardens," the constable said.

The sergeant nodded and scratched something in his book. "It's enough to go on with. Put her in one of the holding cells until we're ready to take her over to the magistrate."

The constable took her to an iron barred cell that already held several women, who could have been anything from prostitutes to murderers. It was as cold in there as it had been outside. He took off the handcuffs that held her and pushed her inside. Kaia pressed her back against the cold brick of the wall, looking around herself in fear.

"First trouble with the law?" a woman of perhaps forty in a gaudy red and green dress called over, obviously enjoying Kaia's discomfort. "It shows. I can always tell the new ones. They have that innocent, scared rabbit look to 'em."

"Leave her be, Maisie," another, slightly younger, woman said. She was sitting on a low bench. The half dozen others in the cell looked at her sullenly for speaking.

"Got to have what fun I can before they send me off to Pentonville, haven't I?" the first one said with a cackling laugh. "It's all right for you, Mary. *You're* just looking at a fine."

"Which I'll have to work more to pay off, which will see me back here," the younger woman complained. "And no one *made* you hit that copper."

"Bloody peelers," the older woman said. "What about you, girl, what did you do? Sell yourself on the wrong street, was it?"

Kaia blushed at that suggestion. "I'm not… I don't…"

"So what, then?" the woman said. She waved a hand. "Don't worry, we've all sorts in this cell so far. Couple of thieves, couple of whores, a stabbing…"

"I didn't do anything," Kaia said. "They think I was trying to steal, but I didn't."

"Won't make much of a difference," the younger woman, Mary, said. "Once the coppers say you did it, the magistrates tend to listen. Just have to hope they drag you up in front of a generous beak."

"They said something about 'Old Colston,'" Kaia said, shuddering slightly as she remembered what the constable had said about him being a hanging judge. Still, maybe he'd just been trying to scare her.

"Oh," Mary said. "That's... not good. Maisie, if we're up in front of him, that might mean..."

"I *know* what it might mean," Maisie shot back, a little too loudly. Kaia could hear the fear there under her bluster.

She knew then that this magistrate was going to be everything the constable had said he would be, that he wouldn't listen to her, and that he would probably send her off for transportation as soon as look at her. The thought of that was enough to bring with it, not just fear, but actual panic. She rattled at the bars of the cell as if it might somehow come open and let her free.

"Stop that," Maisie said. "There's no point to it. They're not going to let you just scarper, are they? When you can't change anything, it's better to just wait."

"They have to realize that I didn't do anything," Kaia said.

The older woman shrugged. "Can't rely on them for that. Can't rely on anyone for anything. People always find a way to hurt you or let you down."

Kaia didn't know what to say to that. It wasn't as if she had any way to argue the opposite, from whatever parents had abandoned her, to the Garrows, to the other children in the orphanage, it wasn't as if she could remember anyone being kind to her for her own sake.

Without anything to say, she didn't say anything. She just sat there in the cell, waiting for whatever would happen next, and trying not to let the terror of what it might be show on her face.

*

Kaia sat in the cell, shivering. She was one of the last ones there now. They'd already taken Maisie and Mary. She was alone there, feeling the pulsing of her heartbeat as she waited for her turn.

When it came, it was still too soon. The sergeant walked up to the cell, turned his key, and stood there expectantly with a pair of handcuffs in his hand.

"Come on, time to go. Move yourself, girl."

Kaia stepped out on leaden feet, holding out her hands for the cuffs. She couldn't do it, though. She couldn't just stand there and let this man drag her off to a fate that filled her with horror. No, she couldn't. She *wouldn't*. More than that, she saw her chance.

Kaia forced herself to walk normally until she got to the sergeant, out of the cage.

"You'll be all right, girl. He'll probably transport you rather than hang you."

Was that meant to be a consolation? Without hesitating, Kaia darted left, out towards the entrance. She made it back into the entry hall, only to find a pair of constables there, waiting by the desk.

"Grab her!" the sergeant called out behind her.

Kaia darted for the exit, but the constables reacted faster than she thought they might. They grabbed her arms, trying to wrench them behind her.

"Let me go!" Kaia cried out. "Get off me!"

She fought back with all the wildness she could muster. Mrs. Garrow had always stressed demure, polite behavior, but this was no time for anything like that. Kaia kicked and thrashed, trying to break free. She fought so hard that the sleeve of her dress tore away, but the constable on that side just took a grip on bare skin instead.

Between them, the two constables bore her to the ground, so that the cold tiles of the floor pressed against her cheek. The sergeant stood over her, looking red faced with either exertion or anger.

"Thought you could get away, did you? Well, we'll soon teach you not to-"

"Sergeant," a man's voice said, and the note of command in it was enough that the sergeant went still. Kaia did too, for a moment at least. She looked up, and up, at a tall, slender man who was not wearing the uniform of a police officer, but was instead wearing a dark overcoat and a hat somewhat shorter than the top hats the police uniforms required. His features were sharp, and Kaia had the impression of a kind of fierce intelligence looking out at the world and trying to make sense of it.

The strangest thing was the slight look of puzzlement that came when this man looked at her. He stared at her like she was a problem he couldn't solve, like she intrigued him. In turn, that made Kaia want to know who he was, and why the sergeant was suddenly staring at him with respect.

"Inspector?"

"I don't think it takes two large men to pin down one young woman, do you?" His tone had an arch edge to it, but still, Kaia was grateful for it as the grips of the constables slackened slightly.

"She tried to abscond, sir."

"And what crime is she accused of?" the man asked.

"Petty larceny, sir. We were just about to take her to the magistrate."

The inspector nodded, seemingly more to himself than to the men. Again, Kaia had the impression that he was intrigued by her. "I see. Well, that can wait. For now, let her up please."

The constables hesitated for a second, but then at a look from the inspector did what he asked. It occurred to Kaia that she could run again, but the weight of the inspector's gaze seemed to hold her in place.

"What is your name?" he asked. Unlike the sergeant, this wasn't some officious demand, simply a request.

"Kaia… sir," she said, remembering the trouble with the sergeant.

"There's no need to call me sir, Kaia," the inspector said. "I am Inspector Pinsley. Please come with me, Kaia. I need to talk to you."

CHAPTER FIVE

Inspector Pinsley escorted the young woman as politely as he could to one of the rooms used as an office. He walked slightly behind her, watching her and trying to understand as much as he could. Walking there also meant that he was ready if she tried to run again. Pinsley might not be as heavy handed as some of the constables, but he was no fool, either, and right now, the girl was too important to let out of his sight.

His office was small and white walled, with a slightly wormy wooden cabinet for files and some shelves which currently held nothing but dust and a couple of small books on regulations. They were the minimum Superintendent Hutton had been able to get away with allowing him. A stand on which his official blue uniform coat and top hat sat were a reminder from the superintendent of just how little he liked the idea of plain clothes officers. A part of Pinsley actually appreciated the emptiness of the space, though; it gave him room to think.

There were chairs set on either side of the table, although since both were hard and uncomfortable, Pinsley had never been entirely certain which was meant to be for the inspector and which for those visiting him. Picking the one that put his back to the wall, he gestured to the other.

"Please, take a seat."

The young woman sat down and looked at him as if wondering what fresh trouble she might be in. Pinsley considered her. She was perhaps seventeen or so, slender in a way that suggested she had not been fed enough for much of her life, with golden hair untamed by a bonnet in the way that would have been proper. Her features were delicate, with large blue eyes and a relatively small nose, but it was the seriousness of her expression that caught Pinsley's attention. She was watching him as closely as he watched her.

Then, of course, there was the mark on her arm, revealed by her torn dress in her scuffle with the constables. It stood out darkly against her skin, and this close, Pinsley could see that it was the same as the one on Tabitha Greene's arm.

"I will have one of the constables fetch food," Pinsley said.

"Why?" Kaia shot back. "What do you want?"

Pinsley raised an eyebrow at that sudden suspicion. "Tell me, which orphanage are you from?"

The girl gasped, stood up as if she might make another run for it, and sat down again, staring at him as if he'd just performed some feat of mind reading. It was a look Pinsley was used to.

"How did you..." Kaia began.

"You're suspicious of strangers, and yet clearly not dirty enough to be living on the streets. You were brought in for larceny, but in a place no real thief would be foolish enough to steal. Your dress is cheap and uniform, lacking the touches that might mean living with your family, yet does not appear to be one of those associated with a workhouse or a reform school. You gave no last name to the desk sergeant. The combination suggests an orphanage."

He saw her swallow in obvious fear.

"I won't go back," she said. "I'm seventeen. You can't send me back."

"That is not why I brought you in here," Pinsley said. He could hear her fear, and wanted to reassure her on that point, at least.

"Then why tell me all of that?" Kaia replied.

"So that you will know that I will see it if you lie," he said.

"I *didn't* steal anything," Kaia said. "If you can see if I lie, that's the truth. I didn't."

Pinsley frowned, because she sounded sincere in that, and he had no wish to see an innocent girl in trouble.

"If you help me, I will do what I can to help you," Pinsley promised. Letting go a thief to catch a murderer was a trade his superiors would be more than happy with.

Even so, he could see Kaia's hesitation, and that said a lot about what her life before must have been like, and how little she trusted authority. It had to be more than a minute before she finally nodded.

"All right," she said.

He stared at her arm, bared by the struggle with the constables, and the reason that he had taken her aside like this. The mark there was impossible to ignore. "Tell me, what do you know about that mark on your arm?"

"I… what?" Kaia said. She looked at it. "I don't understand. Why do you want to know about my birth mark?"

"It *is* a birth mark?" Pinsley asked, even though he knew that it was. Dr Florian had confirmed that much. "Not a tattoo, or a brand, or anything of that sort?"

Kaia shook her head. "Not that I remember."

"That is… interesting," Pinsley said. Any of those things might have pointed to a tattooist to find, or a group wanting to mark their own. "And what if I were to tell you that earlier, I saw the same mark on the body of a dead woman?"

He watched Kaia's reaction. The surprise seemed genuine, her hand going to her mouth, her eyes widening slightly.

"I don't know anything about a dead woman," Kaia said.

"I believe you," Pinsley said, wanting to reassure her. "And yet, I also find it improbable that the two of you would be unconnected. Tell me, what do you know of your family?"

"Nothing," Kaia said, shaking her head.

Pinsley was no acolyte of Lavater's ideas on physiognomy, yet he read other works, suggesting that paying enough attention to the subtle cues of behavior could give him a sense of when people were telling the truth. The trick was not in some shifting of the eyes, or motion of the hands, but in all of it, seeing how small behaviors and expressions differed from the normal.

Based on that, Kaia seemed sincere, and that was a puzzle in itself.

"Not even their name?"

"Nothing," Kaia repeated. "If I knew who they were, I would have gone to them."

"A valid argument," Pinsley agreed. "And yet, the likelihood of a connection remains, and I can think of only one way to test that."

"What way?" Kaia asked.

Pinsley looked her over, trying to guess at whether she would be strong enough for this. In truth, though, did that matter? This was someone accused of being a thief, a criminal. Pinsley had to be hard about this. Still, he could hardly believe that he was asking what he asked next…

"Tell me, young lady, how strong is your stomach?" He asked, getting up and lifting down his uniform coat.

That earned him another one of those worried looks in response. "Why?"

Pinsley passed her the coat.

"Because I think I need you to do something rather unladylike," Pinsley said. "I need you to look at a corpse with a mark just like the one on your arm."

*

They travelled by hansom cab, and Kaia had never ridden in a cab before. On the rare occasions she and the others had needed to go out of the orphanage, to church mostly, they'd had to walk in a long line, whatever the weather.

She huddled tighter in the inspector's coat. It was too big for her, and the official blue of it looked incongruous wrapped around her, yet it was warm, and Kaia was grateful for that.

"Why did you give me your uniform coat?" Kaia asked.

"You needed a coat," the inspector replied. "And since my superintendent likes to complain that I do not wear it, I felt that it could see some use."

The cab bounced along at speed, letting her see the expensive town houses of the city as they passed. Each one was tall and square windowed, pin neat and with wrought iron railings outside. The cab itself was a simple space that felt far too confined, yet Kaia consoled herself with the thought that at least it was better than being dragged in front of a magistrate might be.

She looked out of the side of the cab, trying to work out if it might just be best to jump from it, out into the city. Maybe she could get away and not have to rely on the largesse of some policeman she'd just met.

Several things stopped her. One was the speed that the cab was rolling along at, so that if she dove out, she might break bones against the cobbles below. Another was the look on the inspector's face every time Kaia glanced his way, as if he knew exactly what she was thinking. Even the coat she wore worked against her escaping, because it would mark her out among any crowd. Possibly, that was part of the point of it.

The thing that really kept her there, though, was what Inspector Pinsley had hinted at. He'd said that this body they were going to see had a mark like hers, but how could that be? It didn't make sense, when Kaia had never seen a similar mark on someone's skin. Just the prospect of it raised a kind of hope in Kaia that it *might* be connected to her after all. Maybe she might learn something about herself.

The cab pulled up in front of a hospital, and Inspector Pinsley alighted, giving Kaia his hand to help her down. They headed inside, and a porter moved into their path, but the look Inspector Pinsley gave him stopped him short.

"Is Dr. Florian still in the anatomy theater?" the inspector asked.

"Down in the cellars, sir," the other man said. "Says it's better for the preservation, if you can believe that."

"I can," the inspector said, and led the way, to a set of stairs that led down into a space that was even colder, if anything, than the city outside. Kaia tried to keep pace with him, which wasn't easy given that he was taller and marched along with all the speed provided by long legs.

"Do you know which way you're going?" Kaia asked.

"Yes," Inspector Pinsley said. He paused outside a door which had Dr Florian's name on it, along with an injunction to keep out. He seemed worried, although it was hard to tell against the background severity of his expression. "I should say that what you see in here may be unpleasant."

"You don't need to worry about me," Kaia said.

"Even so…"

"Four years ago, when there was the cholera outbreak?" Kaia said. "Three girls in my orphanage died one night. It would have cost more to remove them before morning, so we had to sit there all night, with their bodies there on the three beds furthest from the rest… Ruth was only ten."

The inspector looked as if he might say something then, but also like he didn't know what *to* say. Instead, he pushed the door open.

The space beyond held simple wooden coffins, along with a stone slab. A man in what looked like a butcher's apron was leaning over something partially shrouded by a sheet, sewing, using a long needle and thread. The cold down here was intense, and Kaia wished that she could put her shiver just then down to just the cold. There was a scent in the air that wasn't strong, but did seep into her nose, refusing to leave. It carried decay and death with it, making Kaia want to back away.

She didn't, though. She didn't want to look weak or scared in front of the inspector, even though that made no sense. She walked into the room with him, and the man by the slab looked round sharply.

"Inspector, you have returned, and… *why* have you brought a young woman with you? This is *not* appropriate. And her attire… with one sleeve hanging off, she should not be here, Inspector."

"She needs to be. I need her to look at the body."

He waved Kaia forward, but Kaia was already stepping up to the slab, staring down at the woman who lay there, dead. For a second, all she *could* do was stare. The sight of it was too overwhelming.

It wasn't the fact that the woman was dead. It wasn't even the stitching marks all over her body, where the doctor had done his work. Kaia had seen worse things than this. This wasn't anything she could put her finger on. Instead, a sense of wrongness rose up through her.

"I need to compare the mark on her arm against your own," the inspector said.

Kaia nodded, but all she wanted to do right then was run. She could see from here that the mark on this woman's body was identical to her own. That fact should have been intriguing, but instead, it only increased her sense of panic. There was something wrong with all this. It made no sense.

The inspector took her arm, staring at the mark there with an intensity that was almost frightening. Kaia could see the puzzlement there on his face, and it matched the confusion she felt.

Who was this woman? *Why* did she have the same mark as Kaia? Since it was a birthmark, did that mean that they were related? Did birthmarks even work like that? Was this her cousin, her aunt, her… mother?

"You're *sure* this is not a tattoo?" Pinsley asked the doctor.

"Quite certain. Nor does it appear to be a birthmark, a brand, or anything else of that nature. Quite what it *is,* I couldn't say."

The mystery of it was enough to hold her there, but everything else told her that she should run. There was something very dangerous here, and without being told, Kaia knew that she was right at the heart of it.

CHAPTER SIX

When they got back to the station, Pinsley's mind was still reeling from what he'd seen with the body. It made no sense, and he needed to think. He led Kaia over to the desk sergeant.

"Is she good to send over to the magistrate now, sir?" the sergeant asked.

Pinsley shook his head. He wanted to make that part clear. "Find somewhere to hold onto her for now. I will still require her later."

"Very good, sir."

"What?" Kaia demanded. "You're just going to throw me back like some fish you've caught? I thought you were going to *help* me."

The sergeant looked as if he might bark something at her, but Pinsley cut him off before he could.

"Not back in with everyone else," he said. He didn't want to just throw her in the cells. "I need her kept safe, for the moment, but I also need space to think."

"Very good, Inspector," the sergeant said, he took Kaia's arm and led her off. She gave him a look of utter betrayal, which Pinsley did his best to ignore. He was doing his best. He could hardly just let her go when he might need her again soon, and he couldn't take her with him, when he needed the peace to think. The sergeant would find a room or something to put her in.

He retreated to his office, where he sat at his desk and reached into one of the drawers. He took out the metronome that sat there and wound it, letting the tick of it in the background chop the air into small pieces with its sound. A clock would do the same job in a pinch, but it wasn't quite the same. The ticking of it was an orderly thing, reminding Pinsley of Catherine practicing at the piano, their daughter by her side. That order made it easier to think.

There wasn't as much to think about here as Pinsley would have liked. Back in the Crimea, the problem had been one of bringing order to the chaos of battle, seeing through it well enough to formulate a suitable plan. Even with most crimes, the problem was usually cutting through the chaos of too much information to the truth beneath.

Here, the problem was a *lack* of information, or at least of the right information. He had the beginnings of a connection in the mark that Kaia and Tabitha Greene shared, but it wasn't enough to untangle the question of how Tabitha had been killed in a locked room, seemingly by some clawed creature.

The link was important. The question was how. More than that, the question was the true nature of that connection. He had hoped that taking Kaia to see Tabitha's body would stir some knowledge in her, break free some measure of understanding. Instead, it had achieved nothing except to distress the girl, however much she tried to hide it.

Pinsley actually felt a little guilty about that, with the guilt tempered only slightly by the knowledge that he had probably saved her from far worse. He found himself thinking about her look of betrayal as he'd sent her off with the sergeant, too. Still the ticking of the metronome brought him back to thoughts of the murder, to reason, to order.

He read what he could on the natural sciences, of course. None of it gave him an answer as to why two people might have identical marks in such a strange pattern, or how to make sense of the way the murder had taken place. A killing through a locked door? A less rational man might be talking about the supernatural, while a less thorough one might take things at face value and assume that Tabitha Greene's roommate had killed her.

Pinsley was neither, and that meant the lack of an answer, in a way that was utterly jarring.

His mind kept drifting back to the girl, Kaia. She was probably no older than his daughter would be now, and yet she had been able to look at a body while flinching as little as some of the officers back in the war had. That saddened him, because it said that too much cruelty had already occurred in her life. He wanted to just let her go, but knew that he couldn't, not yet. Just because she knew nothing, that didn't mean others wouldn't know *her*.

If Pinsley could find someone who knew her, or who recognized the mark, he felt certain that it would help to lead him to the truth. Of course, for someone to recognize Kaia, she would need to be there with him, rather than sitting in a cell.

Pinsley suspected that would not go down well with his superiors. Even though he was convinced of Kaia's innocence, even he was not entirely sanguine about the prospect. After all, his job was to catch criminals and let the courts decide their guilt, not see them released.

He contemplated his options, but the problem with logic was that sometimes it was inescapable. He knew what this situation demanded, and the good that might come from it, just as he knew all the difficulties that might come from doing this. Still, he couldn't see another way.

Pinsley reached out to still the metronome. He'd made up his mind.

*

"You want to do *what,* sir?" the sergeant asked.

"Release the girl into my custody," Pinsley said. "I've already taken her over to see the body."

"This is significantly more… open-ended, sir," the sergeant said.

"Do it, please, Sergeant," Pinsley said. "I'll take the consequences."

"Yes," a voice said behind him, "you will."

Pinsley turned, and had to force a smile at the sight of Superintendent Hutton. He was a man in his fifties, rail thin and with thinning, dark hair. He wore his uniform, of course, the blue of it standing at odds with Pinsley's street clothes.

"What is this about wanting to release a thief, Pinsley?" he asked. His voice always had an edge to it.

"One who I believe to be innocent, sir. She may be able to help with a rather more important matter, in any case," Pinsley said. "The killing at Bedlam?"

"I had understood that to be a simple matter," Hutton said.

"It has… hidden complexities, sir," Pinsley replied.

"And this girl, this arrested thief, is important in trying to unravel them?" Hutton asked.

"Potentially, sir," Pinsley said. It was difficult explaining things to the superintendent, because he reminded Pinsley rather too much of a certain kind of officer he'd run into in the army, listening either to take the best ideas for themselves, or to catch out those they disliked.

So it came as quite a surprise when Hutton turned to the sergeant and waved him towards the cells.

"Very well, Sergeant, fetch her out," Hutton ordered, and the sergeant set off in the direction of the cells.

"Thank you, sir," Pinsley said to the superintendent.

"Don't thank me, Inspector," Hutton said. For a moment, he looked around the room, as if checking that the two of them would not be overheard. "I am not doing this for your benefit."

34

"No, sir?" Pinsley said, in what he thought of as his best talking-to-officers tone: polite, empty, and without a trace of any of the insults he might have shot back in that moment.

For a moment, he thought that Hutton might walk away, but the other man seemed to sense an opportunity to get something off his chest that he'd wanted to say for a while. He walked over to the sergeant's desk, instead, leaning against it.

"I do not like you, Pinsley," he said. "But then, I'm sure you have determined this with your vaunted 'skills of detection.'"

Pinsley saw no reason to lie. "I am aware of it, sir."

"The police force was always meant to be a *civilian* service," Hutton said. "We are not the French, or the Prussians, to have soldiers on the streets. Yet *you* get to come in and take a senior position. Then there is this nonsense of policemen outside their uniforms."

"The use of police in civilian clothes was approved fifteen years ago sir," Pinsley pointed out, in what he hoped was a neutral tone. Disliking one's superior officer was one thing, but letting it show was quite another. "And it is sometimes necessary. I always carry my warrant card and truncheon, as regulations require."

"How can the public have our trust, if they think we might be watching from the shadows?" the superintendent demanded, taking a step forward and putting a finger beneath Pinsley's nose. "No, Pinsley, you represent everything that is dangerous for us. The sooner you are gone, the better."

Pinsley fought the urge to react. Touching the superintendent at this point would be to give him exactly what he wanted.

"If you feel that way, sir," Pinsley said. "I must ask why you have decided to help me in this matter."

"Oh, I'm not helping you, Pinsley," Hutton said. He took a step back from Pinsley and lowered his arm. "If Commissioner Mayne were not such a friend to you, I would simply dismiss you. As it is, I must have cause, and I suspect that this fool's errand will give me exactly that. If not, well, one of my men will have succeeded in catching a killer."

"And you get what you want either way," Pinsley said, with the tightest of smiles.

"Did you think that you were the only clever man in London?" Hutton asked, and then turned on his heel, walking off into the building. He paused, but didn't look back. "I will be watching, Pinsley. Even if you succeed here, do not think yourself safe. The government is collapsing over the whole Orsini business, and a new one may well mean changes for all of us."

Pinsley watched him go, trying to decide if he should feel angry or afraid at his superior's attitude. Ultimately, though, he could summon neither emotion when it came to Superintendent Hutton, only a kind of dull contempt for a kind of man he had come to know only too well in his life.

For now, at least, the commissioner was enough of a friend that Pinsley was safe. Sir Richard Mayne would not allow Hutton to just dismiss him out of hand. As long as he did his job well… no, Pinsley shook his head, refusing to think about it. He was not a man made for the politics of all this. If he had been, perhaps he would have ended his military career at a rather higher rank.

The sergeant came back with Kaia, the girl looking daggers, first at him and then at Pinsley.

"You put me in a *cell*," Kaia said.

Pinsley frowned at that. "Sergeant, where exactly did you put Kaia to keep her safe?"

"The cells, sir, but like you said, I made sure she was confined alone."

"That wasn't what I…" Pinsley knew there was no point in arguing. It didn't matter, just as the politics of the superintendent's dislike didn't.

What mattered was being able to find some link that might help to solve this murder. If, as Pinsley believed, Tabitha Greene's cellmate had played no part in the murder, then the real killer was still out there, free to kill again, or to profit from the murder as they wished. Meanwhile, an innocent woman might hang for it. Pinsley would weather a little displeasure to get to the truth.

"You can't just put me away and bring me out again when it's convenient for you," Kaia said. Pinsley could hear the anger there, but there was worse than that, there was disappointment. To his astonishment, Pinsley found himself reacting to that disappointment, feeling… shame.

"I'm sorry," he said. "It wasn't my intent that the sergeant should put you in a cell."

"Why should I believe that?" Kaia said.

Pinsley shook his head. "I still intend to help you, but I will do whatever I need to in order to solve this murder, first."

"And why should I care?" Kaia said. If looks could have killed, Pinsley suspected that the Yard would have had another murder to solve.

Pinsley cocked his head to one side. "I am sorry, Kaia. Yet the same reasons as before still apply: you are a thief, and if you help me, I will try to help you. More than that, though, you are linked to this in some way. I believe that you want to understand how as much as I do."

"I…" He thought that Kaia might try to deny it, but her lips tightened, biting back the words. She nodded, just once.

"Very well, then," Pinsley said. "Ccome with me."

"Where are we going *this* time?" Kaia asked. "To see another body?"

The answer filled Pinsley with far more worry than that possibility. "To Bedlam."

CHAPTER SEVEN

As she walked from the police station, Kaia considered running again. She didn't care what the inspector had meant or not meant, putting her in a cell; he'd still done it. No sooner had the idea of running come to her though than Pinsley's hand was resting on her arm, escorting her to a hansom cab as delicately as if he'd been chaperoning her around Kew Gardens. Not that Kaia had any real idea what that felt like.

Then again, she'd had no idea what a carriage ride felt like before today, and now she was on her second. The city flew by outside the window, the day already further along than Kaia might have imagined. People out there were going about their business, and because this was Westminster, that business wasn't anything Kaia could really imagine. She stared at them in a state of wonder that she tried to hide from the inspector, because she didn't want him thinking that she was some stupid girl who had seen nothing of the world.

The men walking past in their long frock coats, gaiters and top hats were probably barristers and politicians rather than coalmen or costermongers, although Kaia *did* spot a couple of young sweeps hurrying between the fine townhouses.

Then there were the women, who walked along looking so bright and elegant in their mauve hooped skirts and careful corsetry, their delicate bonnets and their shoes that looked more like slippers in some cases. She was used to men and women in their Sunday best from the orphanage's trips to church, but this was something else entirely. Kaia found herself feeling a little jealous every time their carriage passed them.

"You're not talking to me?" Pinsley asked, as Kaia kept staring out of the carriage's window.

"I've nothing to say," Kaia said, and then realized that wasn't true. She had one very important thing to say, the fear behind it sitting there, refusing to go away. "Back there, you might not have ordered me locked up, but you still handed me over to the sergeant like it was nothing. How do I know that you're not just going to do that the moment I'm done helping you?"

She looked over at him as she said it, although she wasn't sure why she bothered. With a man like this, she might as well have been talking to a wall. To her surprise, though, she thought she saw a trace of guilt on Inspector Pinsley's face.

"I won't do that," he said. "And perhaps… perhaps I was too swift to consign you to the sergeant's care. I needed to think, though."

"And you couldn't have me there for that part?" Kaia asked.

"I needed to concentrate," Pinsley said. "But I am sorry, I did not wish to distress you."

"I am not 'distressed,'" Kaia said, shooting a hard look his way. Would he say that she was hysterical next? "I'm angry."

"You know," Pinsley said, "it is quite rare for a young woman to be quite so… forceful in conversation. Is this how you were back at the orphanage?"

"Are you trying to get me to tell you where I'm from?" Kaia countered, wary of all the ways the inspector might use anything she said against her. The inspector didn't answer, just looked at her instead until the silence expanded too much for Kaia to leave it empty.

"No," she said, "if I spoke to… the people who ran the orphanage, they would have caned me. But they *did* teach me that the only person I can rely on is myself. If I don't speak up for myself, who will?"

Pinsley nodded, as if acknowledging the truth of that. Kaia thought that she could see a trace of sympathy on his face, too.

"I'll say this to you," he said. "I have no interest in sending you before a magistrate, to go to the colonies, or the gallows, or anywhere else. My job is to catch the hardened criminals of this city, not girls who haven't even managed to steal anything."

Kaia frowned at that, not wanting to hope, not *daring* to. "Does that mean that you're planning to let me go?"

"*If* you help me," Pinsley said. "And *if* you don't try to run. I saw the way you were looking around for a way out as we walked to the carriage."

"I…" Kaia looked at him, and she knew in that moment that it would be a very bad idea to lie. "Yes. Do you blame me?"

Pinsley shook his head. "But I shall if you run. I need your help. The mark on your arm is the key to this, I am certain. And in return, I will help you."

Kaia still wasn't sure if she could trust what he said, but she wasn't sure what choice she had.

"You're *really* taking me to Bedlam?"

That was a name to strike fear into anyone. Stories about the madhouse were among the many that Mrs. Garrow had used to terrify them into submission. It was a place people were sent to be forgotten, where they gibbered and lashed out in their madness. Just the thought of going there filled Kaia with dread.

"It's where the murder took place," Pinsley said. "Believe me, I understand your reservations."

"You do?" Kaia doubted that. In fact, she doubted everything he was telling her. Yet he was her best chance of freedom, *real* freedom, because if she ran, she would be looking over her shoulder until she got far away from London. Would Bath be far enough? Liverpool?

Then there was the other part of this. She wanted to find out about whatever linked her with Tabitha Greene. She wanted to find out who she *was*, and that meant only one thing.

"All right," she said. "I'll do what you want, and I won't run."

"Good," Pinsley said, giving no real hint that he felt anything at all about it, beyond whatever small satisfaction there was in her doing what he wanted. That was the part that worried Kaia. She understood that a man like him was meant to be reserved and courteous, just as a girl like her was meant to be demure and obedient. She wasn't sure if that was the way he *actually* was, or if it was all some careful show. Sadly, she didn't possess whatever skills he had for ferreting out the truth from the smallest clues.

Kaia returned her attention to the city beyond the carriage windows instead. There wasn't the fog that there had been in the early morning, giving her a good view as it rolled from Westminster out over one of the bridges, the new version of London Bridge, she thought. It was thronged with people and carts, apparently not put off by the February cold. Below, barges and taller ships seemed to push for space beneath the bridge's arches. In spite of its newness, the bridge was already weather beaten and dirty.

Their cab came out into much more tangled streets that looked far poorer, more like the streets around the orphanage than the kinds of places that might have held lords or ministers.

"Where are we now?" she asked.

"You don't know?" Pinsley replied.

Kaia knew how unlikely it sounded. She'd lived in London for as much of her life as she could remember, after all, but it wasn't as if she'd been allowed out of the orphanage to get a true sense of it. She was as much a newcomer to it as anyone might have been coming in from the countryside. She shook her head.

"Southwark," Pinsley said, although he didn't expand beyond that. Kaia had to look for herself instead.

The buildings on either side looked older than those in the heart of the city, and even if they were well cared for, they didn't have the same edge of brightness or wealth to them. People and horses were moving through the streets, some going to unload goods from barges on the river.

The streets were packed on every side. There were already people stumbling out of public houses and eateries, while hawkers tried to attract people into shops. Kaia watched all of it with the hunger that came from having stared at the inside of an orphanage's walls for far too long.

She spotted Southwark Cathedral over the houses now, the four points of its tower standing over everything around it, while near her, other large buildings started to fill the space around a wide open field with a needle like an obelisk set at its heart. This place was meant to be less wealthy than the space around the police station, yet it was still grander than anything Kaia had known in her life. She couldn't understand how anyone would have the money to build all of this.

Then Bedlam came into sight, and Kaia didn't need Inspector Pinsley to tell her that was what it was. Something about the sight of it made her heart skip a beat in her chest.

It shouldn't have, at first glance. It was large, and square, and almost prettily designed, with two wings coming off a central core the way a country house might have stood. The railings around it and on some of the windows marked it for what it was, though, yet even that wasn't enough to explain the feeling of dread that came over Kaia as she looked at it. This was a place that she didn't want to be.

She *had* to go there, though. She didn't have a choice in it, not unless she wanted to take her chances running, and she knew that she couldn't do that when she still had to find out what the mark on her shoulder meant. That part drew her in as surely as the rest of the place pushed her away with dread.

Their carriage pulled up in front of the building, and they alighted. Kaia stared up at the place, shuddering at it. She half expected

Inspector Pinsley to ask her if she was all right, but his own expression seemed tight, with no room for anything approaching sympathy.

"Let us go in," he said. "The sooner we do this, the sooner we can be done with it."

Kaia nodded, and started towards the door. She had to step to the side as a man came out, though, white-haired beneath his hat, his frock coat a cloudy grey. He walked with the aid of a cane, although he put little weight on it, and carried a doctor's leather case. His features were avuncular beneath a short white beard, his eyes as rheumy and grey as his coat. He should have been a kindly figure, and yet something about him made Kaia shiver with a kind of horrified revulsion as she stepped from his path.

There was something about this man that seemed to go deeper than his skin, something that Kaia could feel without knowing how. It seemed to pour from him, even as he smiled her way and stepped past her. It was something wrong, something completely alien, and Kaia couldn't understand it.

Then he was past her, walking on out into the square beyond, and Kaia had to face something even worse than strange-seeming doctors. She plunged forward, walking willingly into Bedlam.

CHAPTER EIGHT

The man who had once been the doctor had to force himself to walk out into St George's Field without looking back. He could practically feel the eyes of the girl on him, and a part of him expected some attack, some cry of recognition from her.

He certainly recognized what *she* was.

The days before the shadow had been a part of him were hazy things in his memory now. It had been in him only a short time, yet in truth, that period was the only part of his life that seemed real now, somehow.

The doctor was no fool; he knew that a part of that was due to the opium. As a medical man, he knew the dangers of it, and yet just the thought of it made his grip tighten on his cane with the need for it.

No, not now, not yet.

Was the whisper within him the voice of his own thoughts, or was it the shadow? Was there even a distinction, anymore? He was it and it was him, so that there were no neat divisions, no clean understandings, anymore.

He kept walking across the field. Once, he would have taken a cab to return home, but he had the strength to walk it now, and he wanted to enjoy what he could of the day. Besides, if it allowed him to slip into a certain alley in Soho, and knock on a certain door to get what he needed without it going missing from medical stocks...

No, not yet.

A part of the doctor supposed, as he walked back towards London Bridge, that he must be insane. Had another man told him that he was ridden by shadows, that they spoke with his voice and acted with his hands, he would have had them committed to Bedlam for their own safety. At the same time though, the shadow told him that he was not mad, that he was finally seeing the world clearly.

It told him just as clearly that Tabitha Greene had not been mad, although the doctor had been the one to place her in Bedlam anyway. It told him exactly what she was; the knowledge of shadow-seers coming as surely as his understanding of the shadows did.

43

He saw them as he walked, memories of them fresher than those of his life. He could barely remember his time at medical school now, or the face of his wife, or the last novel he had read. Yet he knew things instead about the encroachment of the world of light onto the darkness, and the ways in which it had to be stopped.

He kept walking, and the world looked very different to the one in his memories. *That* world had been a thing of reflected light alone, of brightness and color that made him wince to think about now. Even safely joined to one such as this, so that there was no pain, he could feel disgust at the light, and the brightness, and the... wait, was it him thinking this?

Did the distinction matter? They were one being now, one body, one mind. He stood and looked at his shadow on the ground. He liked to think of it as representing the shadow in him, but he also knew that it was nowhere near that simple. No one looking would be able to tell where the doctor stopped and the shadow began, not even him. Except a shadow-seer.

He needed to focus. The shadow made it easier to think, but still, the need for opium was sending his thoughts rambling. He should be happy right now, not worried. His visit to Bedlam had proved that much. The ones he'd spoken to there had been happy to confirm that they thought the girl, Elsie, had killed Tabitha Greene. They'd scoffed at the thought that it could be anything else. Things were settled there, in exactly the manner they were supposed to be settled. If one mad girl hanged over it... well, there were always more like her. If humanity was anything, it was an endless stream of plenitude, with more and more still brought into the world to replace any lost.

Everything was as it should be, and yet the doctor couldn't help thinking about the girl who had stared at him as he'd left Bedlam. That look... he hadn't liked that look. It had told him what she was as surely as the mark on her arm.

Was she a new patient being brought to the asylum? She had looked wild enough for it, with no bonnet and a torn dress. Perhaps the man with her was there to commit her, perhaps he was a family member, or a doctor like him. The doctor laughed at the thought that there might be anyone quite like him, although the knowledge that came from the shadow told him that there *were* others, many others...

That did not matter, though. The girl, possibly, did. If she was being given over to Bedlam's care, that potentially made things easier. If not, then it might be necessary to take other steps. Either way, the situation was one that the doctor would have to monitor, as carefully as he might once have monitored a patient, or measured out the dosage of opium.

No, it was no use, he had to go. He waved over a cab, because walking wouldn't get him what he wanted quickly enough. Hopping in, he settled back in the seat.

"To Soho," he told the driver. "Quickly now."

The man cracked the reins and they set off. Soon, the doctor would have what he needed. After that... well, he would see how things stood with the girl, and he would act appropriately. The shadow would make sure he did.

CHAPTER NINE

From the moment they arrived at Bedlam, Pinsley could see how nervous Kaia was. Why, she practically jumped out of her skin as a doctor came past, presumably after visiting some patient or other. He found himself wondering if she would be able to do this, which at least made it easier to ignore his own misgivings about the place.

"Let's go in," he said, opening the door and holding it for her until she stepped inside.

The most that he could say for the place was that it was marginally less disturbing in daylight. The large, central lobby looked a little less forbidding: a little more like a hospital and a little less like a prison. By daylight, it was possible to make out the portrait of the queen sitting behind the main desk, and a number of other paintings hanging on the walls. Still, those weren't exactly reassuring; several of them had an odd, disjointed quality to them that suggested they might have been produced by the patients. The sounds of those patients shouting, crying out, and occasionally screaming in the distance made it abundantly clear what this place was, and Pinsley had to remind himself that these were simply people who needed help. He found himself thinking of his aunt, and steeled himself for everything within.

The asylum's warden sat behind the desk, and to Pinsley, it looked as if he hadn't slept. He obviously remembered Pinsley too, because the man gave him an annoyed look.

"I didn't think you'd be back, Inspector. Surely you have concluded your business here?" He looked over in Kaia's direction. "Unless you have come to bring us a new inmate? I have received no notice of such a thing, though."

"Kaia is not here as a prisoner, but as someone who may be able to help me with my inquiries," Pinsley said.

"A new inspector, perhaps?" the warden joked. "Your superiors will not like a mere girl wearing a policeman's coat."

"I suspect that they would like it less if she were to freeze in the February air," Pinsley shot back. He disliked this man. There was something too amused with himself about him. "As for the conclusion of my business, I find that murder inquiries are best concluded only once the murderer has been apprehended."

The annoyance on the warden's face gave way to something harder. "The murderer does not need to be apprehended, because she already sits in our custody. The girl, Elsie, is quite clearly the killer. Who else could it be?"

"That remains to be determined," Pinsley said. "The wounds do not support such a thing, though, and nor does the lack of a weapon. I need to speak with her again, and with the other inmates close by."

"Because the testimony of the insane is of such use?" the warden shot back. He tapped the bulk of the visitors' book. "Oh, very well. Sign in, and be about your business."

Pinsley let Kaia sign in first. He could see her hand shaking, and wanted to reach out to comfort her, but knew that wasn't his place. She was a witness, not his daughter. When it came to his turn signed his name in the visitors' book, and took the opportunity to scan its pages again for information. Still, nothing leapt out at him, it was all just normal records of comings and goings: visitors there to see the patients, orderlies arriving and leaving. Still, no visitors for Tabitha Greene had magically appeared since this morning. Indeed, going back through the log book, it seemed that no one had been to see her for some time.

"Is it usual, for your inmates to have so few visitors?" Pinsley asked. It seemed sad that someone should be so alone in such a place.

The warden shrugged. "It depends who they are. We have an artist in the men's wing, Dadd, and people come from far and wide to see him. Others find that they are alone, with even their families not wanting to see them."

"Why would someone's family just abandon them?" Kaia asked, at Pinsley's side. "How could someone just do that?"

"Would *you* visit someone whose mind is hopelessly lost, young lady?" the keeper countered. "Would you want to see someone you had cared about turn into something unrecognizable, likely with no hope of things changing for the better?"

Pinsley wished he could argue with that, but again, he found himself thinking of his aunt. As a boy, he'd been terrified of going to see her. Could he blame others for thinking the same way?

"You don't do anything to help them?" Kaia asked.

"We contain them," the warden said. "We provide a calm, controlled environment. We provide rational, beneficial tasks for our inmates, with rewards and punishments to encourage sane, civilized

47

behavior. Beyond that, what would you *have* us do? Do away with restraints as some have? Those who have lost control of their moral faculties must have strict discipline to encourage them to regain them. Inspector, if you have business, please take this girl and be about it. I will not have my methods questioned by those who clearly lack understanding."

"Come on, Kaia," Pinsley said, leading the way towards the room that held Elsie. One of the keepers there let them through the barred gates and led them as they kept going, deeper into it.

Now that it was daylight, more of the inmates were out in the hallways, moving round from one spot to another, talking to one another, occasionally laughing for no reason, or just sitting there in the corners. There was plenty of strange behavior. Some danced to songs only they could hear, while others cried out, or bellowed obscenities. A few were chained even though such things had supposedly gone out of use in other places a decade or more ago. Here and there, visitors stared at them, apparently treating the show as they would have a music hall performance.

"This place is vile," Kaia said. "It's… oppressive."

Pinsley could only agree. The whole place might have been designed as something lighter and more airy than the old Bedlam, but there was no kindness here. If things had moved on from the days when his aunt had faded in such a place, he could not see how.

"I am sorry to bring you here," he said. "But we must have answers."

He went to Elsie's room, and she was there. She had no choice in the matter. Unlike most of the others there, she was locked in, and when the keeper opened the door, Pinsley saw that she had also been fastened into the confines of a straightjacket. She looked up in fear as Pinsley, Kaia, and the keeper stepped into the room.

"Get her out of that restraint," Pinsley ordered the keeper.

"Sir, the instructions regarding this prisoner were quite clear. She killed someone."

"That is what *I* am determining, not you," Pinsley said, injecting the full force of his authority into the words. "Now do as I have asked, and leave us alone."

The keeper did so, backing away hurriedly. Pinsley wasn't looking at him, though, because his attention was on Elsie. She was sitting curled up on the bed, hardly daring to look at them.

"Elsie," Pinsley said. "Elsie, do you remember me?"

48

"No, I…" her voice had an almost dreamlike quality to it. "Wait, you were here before. You were here when…"

She pressed herself back to the wall, shaking her head over and over.

"I didn't do it. I didn't."

"I believe you," Pinsley said, moving to crouch in front of her. As before, everything about her said that she was telling the truth. More than that, Pinsley had physical evidence now: this young woman was too slight and short to have inflicted the injuries on Tabitha Greene's body.

She looked at him like she wasn't quite sure whether to trust that, or not.

"I believe you," Pinsley repeated. "I know that you are no killer."

"That's… thank you," she said. Pinsley could see tears in her eyes. "No one believes me."

"I know," Pinsley said. "I'm hoping that I can find the real killer, and make this right."

She shook her head at that, muttering to herself.

"The shadows… there was a shadow…"

"Elsie, I came back because I want you to meet someone," Pinsley said. He waved Kaia forward. "Her name is Kaia. She has a mark on her arm that is very similar to one on Tabitha's. Show her, Kaia."

Kaia did it, and Pinsley wasn't sure what he had hoped for in that moment. That this young woman would somehow recognize something in Kaia's face, or in the mark? That the sight would shake loose some pertinent piece of information?

Instead, Elsie started shaking. "Tabitha. There was so much blood. So much blood. The shadow came in. A shadow, and there were claws. I swear… I…"

She went quiet, almost folding in on herself as if huddling there would stop any of this from touching her. In that moment, Pinsley knew that he'd done the wrong thing, coming here.

He reached out a hand, putting it on her arm to comfort her. All he'd done by bringing Kaia here was to distress both her and Elsie.

"I am sorry to have disturbed you, Elsie," Pinsley said, standing and making for the door.

"Please," Elsie almost whispered as he reached it. "Please don't let them hurt me anymore. I didn't… I can't…"

"No one is going to hurt you for this," Pinsley promised her. "If you are as innocent of this as I believe you to be, you have nothing to fear."

"Thank you," she said.

Pinsley and Kaia stepped out into the corridor.

"You were kind with her," Kaia said, as they stepped out into the corridor. Pinsley heard the surprise there. The keeper was waiting to re-lock the door.

"Do you think me incapable of kindness?" Pinsley replied. The fact that Kaia didn't answer straight away was a kind of answer in itself. "It is hard to be kind, sometimes, given my job. I'm here to find out the truth, Kaia, and I will. I will be kind if I can, but I will also do what I must to find that truth."

It was as much a promise to himself as a statement to Kaia. He would find a way to piece together the reason of this.

"You should stay close," he said. "We need to ask the others here if they have remembered anything."

Pinsley went to the other rooms there. Most were open during the day, and a few still had women sitting or lying in them. Going to one across the way, he knocked, and found a woman there sitting in only layers of petticoats, staring into space.

"Who are you?" she demanded.

"Inspector Pinsley, ma'am, of the metropolitan police."

"That's what you would say. I don't know you."

"No," Pinsley agreed. "I have not met you before, but I would like to ask you some questions…"

"I don't *know* you!" the woman shouted. "Get out. Get out!"

She kept shouting until Pinsley and Kaia backed away from the room. Pinsley went to the next room, where at least the inhabitants were properly dressed, but of the two women sitting there, one was staring blankly at the wall, while the other was singing an off kilter tune to herself that seemed to worm its way into Pinsley's head.

"Excuse me, ladies," he said. "I am Inspector Pinsley. I need to ask you some questions about the events of last night."

"The killing?" the one who'd been singing to herself asked, in a surprisingly normal sounding voice. "When dear Elsie butchered her friend? Oh, don't look so shocked, man. I know everything."

"You do?" Pinsley asked.

50

"I do," the woman said. "I see everything everywhere, you see. I know everything. It's how I know that the one responsible for this is…"

"Yes?" Pinsley said.

"The queen, of course! Or not the queen, because the one sitting on the throne is an imposter. They won't tell us the truth, but…"

Again, Pinsley found himself backing away.

"There's nothing here," Kaia said. Pinsley caught her glance towards the exit, and he could more than understand it. Rationality was the foundation of his whole existence. Being in a place like this was almost physically painful.

"I know you want to leave," Pinsley said. "But we can't, just yet."

"Why not?" Kaia asked. She shuddered, and Pinsley got the impression that she was maintaining her composure only with an effort. "Why can't we just *go*?"

"Because I still have a job to do," Pinsley insisted. "The inmates might not know anything, but the keepers might, or there might be something in the records of this place. I have to be thorough. There has to be *something*."

There had to be, because if there was nothing, then there was only the insanity of this place, and Pinsley could *not* give in to that. He *would* find a solution, and that meant plunging still deeper into Bedlam.

CHAPTER TEN

"This way, Kaia," Inspector Pinsley said, back to being as unrelenting as always. He'd shown so much kindness to the young woman they'd come to see, yet with her it seemed to be all about what he could learn. When he was done with her, would he really let her go?

Kaia could barely resist the urge to run out of there. Everything about this place was too much, with madness on every side of her. It was a place that she couldn't make sense of. Worse, she didn't even really understand why she was there; it wasn't like anyone had recognized either her or the mark on her arm.

That wasn't what made her want to run, though. The urge was deeper than that, pulsing through her in a danger warning she couldn't pin down. All she knew was that there was darkness everywhere she looked, a sense of wrongness that pervaded the whole building, pressing down on Kaia until it felt as if she couldn't breathe.

For now, though, she had no choice except to follow him. He led the way through the wing, and Kaia could see the women there mostly being ignored and abandoned, except when they did anything that didn't count as normal in the eyes of the keepers. Kaia saw one go up to a woman who was huddled down in a corner weeping.

"Stop that!" he ordered, dragging her to her feet. "If you can't behave properly, then you'll have to go back to your room."

"No, no, I'll…" The woman's words dissolved into tears. "He attacked me. He attacked me. Apples!"

"I've told you about this before," the keeper said. "You can't go around making things up, Margaret."

"He *attacked* me!" she shouted in the keeper's face, waving bruised arms at him.

"That's enough," the keeper said, and started to drag her away. "You'll spend the rest of the day locked in. Maybe that will teach you to stop this nonsense."

Kaia winced at it. Things here were like some worse version of the orphanage, where any little infraction had been punished, trying to crush any independence of spirit left in the girls there. Here, it seemed as if the same approach was being applied in the hopes of driving the madness out of the inmates, as if merely forcing them to behave like everyone else was enough. That seemed crueler still, when so many of the women there had no hope of controlling what they did.

"You should stop them," Kaia said to Pinsley.

"How?" the inspector asked. A note of sympathy crept into his face as he kept walking. "I don't like this any more than you do, Kaia, but there are limits to what I can do. I cannot change the whole of Bedlam, but I *can* try to find Tabitha Greene's killer."

Kaia felt a surge of disappointment at that. If the police couldn't make things better, what was the point of them? She glanced back towards the woman, who was being led back to her cell.

"How do you plan to find a killer when no one remembers anything?" she asked.

"There will be something," Pinsley said. "There *has* to be an explanation for the wounds on her body, and why no knife was found in spite of the door being locked."

"I don't see how," Kaia said. "It makes it sound like some kind of ghostly beast attacked her, something out of a story."

Pinsley shook his head. "The uncanny might make for entertainment, but it is no basis for police work. The world is a rational thing, and there will be a rational explanation for this."

He sounded certain, and Kaia found herself wishing that she could feel that way. The sheer oppressiveness of the asylum around them, though, made it far too easy to believe in things beyond any human reality. This was not a place where the inspector's logic and reason held sway; he'd admitted as much himself.

Kaia was more than grateful when they left the women's wing of the asylum, heading back into the central part, where things were a little cleaner and calmer by comparison. Inspector Pinsley was still marching forward at a brisk pace, so that Kaia had to almost run to keep up. When he reached the front desk, he stepped past the warden there, heading for a flight of stairs.

"Where do you think you're going?" the warden demanded.

"I need to see your records," Pinsley said. "All of them. The visitors' book is a start, but it is not enough. I need to see everything you have."

"And you have a warrant from a magistrate for that?" the warden demanded.

"This is a murder inquiry," Pinsley replied. "I believe you are very familiar with inquiries. Tell me, what do you think would happen if I were to place a report before the Home Secretary about conditions in this place?"

"We would be commended for our commitment to containing difficult and dangerous individuals," the warden said, but even Kaia could hear the nervousness in his voice.

"And *I* am committed to catching a murderer," Pinsley said. "To do that, I require your assistance."

"Damn you," the warden said, and then waved a hand at the stairs. "Very well, I'll have a keeper show you to our records, but I don't know what you think you'll find. Applewood!"

A man came hurrying down from above. He was dressed more like a clerk than like one of the other keepers there, in a severely cut suit of dark grey, although he was larger and more muscled than most clerks might have been. He wore small round spectacles, and had dark, slicked back hair. When he peered across at Kaia, there was something disconcerting about the way his gaze travelled over her.

No, it wasn't just that, although that was more than bad enough. It wasn't even that something clicked in Kaia's mind then, so that apples became Applewood, and she knew who the young woman had been shouting about. It was more than all of that. Looking at him, it was as if she could see all the way through to some dark stain on his soul, without knowing how. Something in her recoiled just at the sight of him, and she knew in that moment exactly how the woman before had come by the bruises on her arms. The thought of it sickened her.

"I'll show you up," the keeper said, and set off for the stairs.

Kaia found herself following in Pinsley's wake once again, half convinced that he wouldn't even notice if she wandered off. A part of her actually *wanted* to hang back, if only to keep away from the disconcerting presence of the asylum keeper. Still, she kept going, because she didn't want the inspector thinking that she was trying to run.

Together, they headed up into a space that seemed to be offices and apartments for those of the keepers who stayed on site, including the warden. This area, Kaia couldn't help noticing, was much cleaner and neater than the rest of it, even insulated from some of the sounds of the mad house below by thickly carpeted floors.

The warden led the way to a room with shelves running round it, and wooden cabinets to hold papers standing at each corner.

"Here are our records," Applewood said. "Can I help you to find something in particular?"

"We don't need your help," Kaia said, more sharply than she probably should have.

"Is this girl in charge of your investigation, Inspector?" the keeper asked.

"No," Pinsley said, giving Kaia a warning look. "Tell me, Mr. Applewood, did you see or hear anything last night that was out of the ordinary?"

"In *Bedlam,* Inspector?" the keeper said with a laugh that was far too friendly. Kaia hated him for that. She could see what he was, so why couldn't the inspector, with all his skill in observation?

"Was anyone here who should not have been?" Pinsley asked.

"No, of course not," the keeper said.

"And no one has found the knife that they believe was used to kill Tabitha Greene?"

"Not that I know," the keeper said, spreading broad, spatulate hands. "I was nowhere near any of it. I was up here, asleep. Some of us keepers stay here, you see, to keep an eye on things."

"And yet that eye saw nothing," Pinsley observed. "Very well, you may go."

The man left, and Kaia glared after him.

"You should arrest him," she said.

"For what?" Pinsley asked, moving to the shelves of records and starting to sort through them.

"He's *obviously* the one who attacked that woman downstairs."

"Based on a half heard word from a madwoman that might or might not have been his name?" Pinsley said. He obviously caught Kaia's small sound of surprise. "Yes, I heard it too, but what I hear and what a magistrate might believe are two different things. It is not enough, you understand? However much I might wish it to be, it is not enough."

"It's more than that," Kaia said. "There's something wrong about him, something dangerous. Can't you *feel* it?"

Pinsley kept sorting through records. He seemed to move with the mechanical precision of a steam engine, picking one up, scanning through it, and putting it down again.

"As a rational man, I do not have the luxury of relying on my feelings to understand the world," Pinsley said. "I require evidence." He started to read out what he found. "Transfer of a prisoner to Harrogate. Note from a doctor. Records of food bought."

He continued to sort through the documents there, while Kaia found herself all but ignored once again. She was starting to suspect that the inspector did not do it deliberately, but simply focused in so tightly on his investigation that there was no room for anything else.

"I could help you look," Kaia said. "What are you searching for?"

"Anything relating to Tabitha Greene, or to last night more generally."

"All right," Kaia said, and went over to the files, which were either written in hardbound books or stored in envelopes between them. There was, at least, a kind of system to them, so that she was able to pull out a file with Tabitha Greene's name on relatively quickly.

"I found this," she said, holding it up for Pinsley to see. "It has an address for her, and notes on her case." She read parts of it to herself. "It says here 'the patient claimed to see the abnormal movement of shadows around peoples, and made additional claims that people were possessed. Upon further questioning, she made allegations against the keepers, saying that they were part of a plot against her.'"

"The nature of her condition is of less interest than notes on who might have seen her and when," Pinsley said. He kept sorting through the files. Occasionally he paused and made notes in a small notebook with a pencil. He stopped, and picked up one particular sheet of paper. "Aha."

"Aha?" Kaia said. "What does 'aha' mean?"

"In this case, it means that I might have to have a conversation with Mr. Applewood after all," Pinsley said. He turned the piece of paper so that Kaia could see it, and she realized after a second or two that it was a schedule of some kind, setting out who was meant to be on duty in which part of the asylum.

In the slot designated for the previous evening in the women's wing, the word "Applewood" stood out clearly.

"So we go to speak with him now?" Kaia asked.

Pinsley appeared to think for a moment. "*I* will speak with him. I would like you to wait outside, please, Kaia. I do not believe that this part is something a young lady should have to witness. There may be… some coarseness."

Kaia wanted to tell him that she could handle anything, but right then she wanted nothing more than to be out of that place. She nodded.

"I'll wait."

"And Kaia," Pinsley said. "Please do not run."

CHAPTER ELEVEN

Pinsley waited until Kaia was gone before he went out to find the keeper, Applewood. Some things were best done without an audience. He took the schedule with him, folding it neatly and placing it in the breast pocket of his overcoat so that his hands would remain free.

It took him a minute or two to find his quarry, back among the rooms reserved for the keepers, sitting in front of a roaring fire, smoking a pipe in a chair as if he were at a club, rather than in the midst of an asylum.

"Did you need something else, Inspector?" Applewood asked.

"I need you to start telling me the truth," Pinsley said.

"Are you calling me a liar, sir?" The keeper surged out of his chair, standing in a rush. "I will not stand for it, when I have been nothing but helpful."

Presumably, the rush of it was intended to get Pinsley to back down. He suspected that with many men, it might even have worked. Applewood was a large man, after all, and no doubt the warden made sure to employ men who could fight, if only to deal with the more dangerous individuals housed at Bedlam.

Pinsley simply stepped back and started to remove his overcoat.

"What's this?" Applewood demanded.

"This is so that I do not tear my coat in the event that you are not forthcoming," Pinsley said. "I have no time for men who would take advantage of defenseless women."

"How dare you!" Applewood said.

"I dare, because I saw the evidence," Pinsley said. "A young woman with bruises from being held down, giving your name as she says that she was attacked."

"The ravings of a mad woman," Applewood snapped back. The keeper took the pipe from his mouth. "I will not stand for being accused like this. You have no evidence. Do you think a court will believe a madwoman?"

No, Pinsley didn't. He'd said as much to Kaia, but that didn't change what they all knew to be true.

He was not usually a man given to anger. Such anger as he had was a colder thing than most men's. Where they might rage and strike out, he had always found himself becoming icier with it, as clear headed as ever, perhaps more so. It had served him well in Crimea, letting him stay calm and plan where others panicked. Now, his veins felt as if they were purest frost.

"I think they might believe the evidence that you are involved in Tabitha Greene's death in some way," Pinsley said.

"What evidence?" Applewood retorted. He seemed to raise his voice every time he spoke, but Pinsley doubted that it would make much of a difference against the background of the asylum's din.

"You lied to me," Pinsley said. "You told me that you had no knowledge of events last night because you were nowhere near it all, yet *you* were the one who was working on that wing."

"You think I'm a killer?" Applewood demanded.

"Why not?" Pinsley asked. "It would have been easy for you to unlock the door, kill Tabitha Greene, and re-lock it when you went. You could hand over to the next keeper, and he would know nothing different. Just tell me… how did you make it look as if a wild beast did this?"

"You're not going to pin this on me!" Applewood cried out. "I won't let you!"

He surged forward, flinging his still lit pipe at Pinsley's face. Pinsley swayed aside from it, then parried a huge overhand punch aimed at his skull.

"You haven't thought this through, Applewood," he said. "Attacking a police inspector? It could go very badly for you."

"I'll say that you were attacked by inmates," Applewood said. "No one will believe you. Nobody *likes* police, especially ones who don't wear their uniforms."

"I won't be believed?" Pinsley said. "It seems to me that you've used that before. Except I am not some helpless young woman. Admit it, Applewood, you played some part in the murder Tabitha Greene. What was it? Would she not keep quiet about your unwanted attentions?"

Applewood roared and threw himself at Pinsley again, swinging wild punches. Pinsley avoided and parried, bringing his arms up to cover when he had to. He stepped forward in a lunging jab that snapped the keeper's head back, making him circle Pinsley more warily.

"It's amazing how many men fancy themselves a Cribb or a Broughton simply because they are large," Pinsley said, "as if that is all there is to prize fighting." He slipped another punch. "Consider Sayer. A hundred and fifty pounds at best, and yet he remains champion of England."

He punctuated the comment with a hook to Applewood's body that drove the air from him in a whoosh.

"Not that I am a hundred and fifty pounds," Pinsley said. "As I think you can tell."

There was a cold sort of enjoyment to this, satisfaction at least, or perhaps the fulfilment of a need he didn't want to acknowledge. A man who hurt women like this one was far too close to the one who had taken Catherine from him. Since *that* killer still didn't have a face in Pinsley's mind, it was all too easy to superimpose Applewood's.

The keeper rushed him, probably assuming that his greater size might tell more at close quarters. It might even have helped, if Pinsley's adjutant back in the war hadn't been a large Lancastrian man named Simms, who had been only too happy to pass on the nastier secrets of that county's style of wrestling. Pinsley tossed the other man over his hip, sending him tumbling to the floor.

Applewood got to his hands and knees, and perhaps another man might have punched him into unconsciousness there and then. There was a clear difference, however, between beating a man who was trying to hurt him and striking one who had no way to fight back. He waited for the other man to get back to his feet.

"Admit what you did," Pinsley said. "After all you've done, have the common decency to do that much. Tell me why you killed her."

"I never killed anyone!" Applewood roared, and he reached out towards the grate of the fireplace. Too late, Pinsley saw him grab a poker from it, the tip glowing red hot.

He lunged at Pinsley with all the speed of a fencer, and even though Pinsley twisted aside from the strike, he wasn't quite fast enough. He felt a moment of burning agony as the tip brushed the skin of his abdomen, but then he had a grip on Applewood's arm, keeping it from him.

He threw the other man to the ground, and wrenched that arm further, twisting until the poker fell to the carpet, smoldering there. For a moment or two, Pinsley stood over the other man, breathing hard.

"I didn't do it," Applewood said. In an instant, his voice had gone from bullying and aggressive to pleading. "I didn't kill anyone, I swear it."

"I believe you," Pinsley said. He was surprised to find that he did. The truth was that this man was too impulsive to plan a murder as baffling as the one the night before had been. Oh, Pinsley could easily imagine him killing someone in a frenzy, but to clean up after himself? To make it so that no one knew that he'd been there? To make it look like some beast had been involved? No, that didn't fit. In any case, if the keeper had possessed a knife big enough to cause the wounds on Tabitha Greene's body, and the nerve to slice such parallel cuts, he suspected that the man would have drawn it by now.

"You believe me?" Applewood said.

"Yes."

"Then why aren't you letting me up?"

"There is still the matter of you attacking young women in your care," Pinsley said, his voice cold. "Vulnerable women with no families to protect them, and no hope of being believed."

He couldn't keep thoughts of his daughter from his mind. Where would Olivia be now? Was she somewhere where she might be at the mercy of a man like this? Was she trying to tell the world who had harmed her, only for them to turn away from her?

"You can't do this," Applewood said. "You've said it yourself, you have nothing. No one will believe someone like her. Not a stupid little-"

Pinsley wrenched his arm hard enough that he heard the snap of breaking bone, and the asylum keeper screamed in pain. Pinsley wished that he could say that there was no satisfaction in that, but that would have been a lie.

"I'll have you arrested!" Applewood cried out. "You can't do this."

"Do what?" Pinsley said. "Stop a man who attacked me when I had not laid a finger on him? Tell anyone, and you'll be facing a noose for attacking a police officer. Or we can agree right now that you fell, like civilized men. Say it."

"I... fell, damn you," Applewood agreed.

"Now, what else do you know?"

"Nothing!" Applewood cried out, as Pinsley put pressure on the broken arm. "Nothing, I swear!"

"Not about movements in the women's wing of the asylum? Not about the reason Tabitha's wounds look so much like they might have been caused by some beast?"

"Nothing!" Applewood insisted. "Curse you!"

"You should learn to keep a civil tongue in your head," he said to the keeper. "And you should learn to keep your hands away from those who are in your care. Forget, and I will be back to break the other arm."

Pinsley stood, leaving the keeper to his agony. He retrieved his overcoat, ignoring the pain in his side from the poker. He covered the wound by buttoning the coat around him. He walked from the room, and headed down through Bedlam, trying to think.

For the briefest of moments, he'd thought that perhaps he had found his murderer. Instead, he'd merely been able to put a stop to a man who abused his position in the vilest ways. He found himself wondering what Kaia would think of that, not that he planned on telling her. The icy anger inside him, left behind by so many of the events of his life, was not a matter for others. If anything, it was a matter for shame, because it showed that all within him was not anywhere near as orderly as he wished.

Better to focus on other things rather than that, such as the question of how Kaia had picked out this man from all the others as the one who had attacked patients. The name was a clue, but something told Pinsley it was more than that; he just didn't know what. It was yet another thing to understand in the tangled web of all of this.

The warden was still behind his desk as Pinsley came down into the lobby. He shot the inspector an unfriendly look.

"That girl of yours went past not long ago," he said. "Without even signing out in the visitors' book. You should consider the company you keep, Inspector."

"And *you* should consider the people you employ more carefully," Pinsley retorted.

That managed to add an extra note of sourness to the warden's expression.

"Get out," the man said.

Pinsley looked around as he turned the collar up on his coat. He took in the cries that still came from deeper in Bedlam, and the all-pervading sense of madness there.

"Only too gratefully," he said, and stepped out of there as quickly as he could.

61

CHAPTER TWELVE

Outside, it was starting to get darker, and Kaia felt stupid standing there in the inspector's overly large coat, but she was still grateful to be out there rather than in Bedlam's depths. That place had a feel to it that went beyond the normal fears of madness or being locked away; something darker sat on the place like an encompassing cloak, and Kaia was grateful to be out from under it.

She was almost as grateful when Pinsley came marching out, as ramrod straight and unyielding as always.

"How did things go in there?" Kaia asked, as Pinsley waved down a cab.

"I had a discussion with Mr. Applewood," the inspector said. "I believe that he has seen the error of his ways."

"A discussion?" Kaia asked. What did that mean? The inspector was so reserved that it was hard to tell what he was thinking, or precisely what he meant.

"Sadly, I do not believe that he is our killer." Pinsley said, as he waved Kaia into the vehicle.

"'ere," the cabbie called down. "I'm not carrying no madwoman."

"The young lady is in full possession of her faculties," Pinsley said. He removed a warrant card and a short brass truncheon from his pockets to indicate his credentials. "And I am about official business. I need you to take us to Great Scotland Yard."

Kaia got into the cab with Pinsley, and started to wait out the ride back to the station. Around them, people were starting to make their way back home. The lamp lighters were starting to make their way around the gas street lamps that stood at intervals. It seemed that everyone in the city had their place in it, even if it was as small a thing as that.

Not her, though. Throughout the visit to Bedlam, she'd felt as if she were only there as an appendage, there to be shown around but not to speak up or *do* anything. Even now, Pinsley seemed to be looking out of the window, thinking, rather than paying any attention to her.

As such, it was quite a surprise when he asked the next question.

"What did you make of things in there, Kaia?"

"You're asking me?" Kaia said. "I thought I was... well, nobody. You could have taken a sketch of me around as easily, for all I got to say or do in there."

Pinsley turned towards her. "If I had done so, I would not have your impressions of the place, and everything that we saw there."

Kaia stopped for a moment, unsure what to say next. The simple fact was that, throughout her life, almost no one had asked her opinion on even the smallest thing. The orphanage was run according to the Garrows' wishes, and those of the girls there didn't come into it.

"Please, Kaia," Pinsley said. "I believe your insights may be valuable. You spotted the danger the keeper presented, after all."

"Do you mean the asylum as a whole?" Kaia asked. She shuddered even at the memory of it. "Because that's... it was too much."

She wanted to say more than that, but she wasn't sure how to. The inspector had made it abundantly clear that he was a man devoted to reason and evidence. How could she start to explain the things that she'd felt at Bedlam, first with the doctor they'd passed, then in the place itself. She would sound mad. She would find herself locked up there the way Tabitha Greene had been...

She wasn't sure where the next thought came from, but as soon as it came to her, Kaia knew that it was an important one.

"What if... what if Tabitha was sent to Bedlam specifically so that she could be murdered?" Kaia said. "The people who sent her would know that if she were to die violently, it would be blamed on the other inmates there. Assuming they could get access to her, it would be the perfect cover for a crime they couldn't commit openly."

For almost the first time since she'd met him, Kaia saw the dispassionate expression on Inspector Pinsley's face change. He seemed... well, he seemed pleased.

"A most impressive thought, Kaia," he said. "And one that potentially provides us with a way to find who might have killed her."

Kaia noted the "us."

"So, you're going to keep me around?" she asked.

Pinsley nodded, but then looked out of the window. "Strictly speaking, I should return you to the station for the night. It is not as if I can take you home with me. I have been staying at my club. It does not permit women entry."

After all this, he was going to take her back *there*?

"Please," Kaia said. "Anywhere but there. I'll sleep under a bridge rather than go back there."

Pinsley seemed a little taken aback by that. He seemed to think for a moment or two. "There may not be a need for something so drastic. There is one place. Driver? A change of plans. Take us to Camden Town, please. St Michael's."

"Right you are, Guv."

They drove across London, back north over the river, then out through Soho, where every gin house and theater was already advertising its entertainments. They headed through Marylebone, the streets turning back to wealthier rows of townhouses, then kept going. Kaia could see a vast expanse of open ground in the distance, tree lined and railed to prevent people coming in now that it was night.

"Regent's Park," Pinsley said, obviously catching her rapt look. "For someone brought up in London, you seem oddly amazed by it."

"I was brought up in one orphanage in London," Kaia said. "We never got to see places like this. We never went north of the river. We barely went more than a street or two away."

In the last day or so, she'd seen more of the city than in the rest of her life put together. Now, she was in a part of London she didn't know, driving past houses that seemed to mix three story town houses with smaller, more soot stained places. A railway line stood between the area and the park beyond.

"They say Camden Town was meant to be an extension of the park," Pinsley said. "Ten years ago, it was quite the up-and-coming area, before the line to Euston, of course. Still, it is a place that has... friends of mine."

The cab came to a halt in front of a small church that looked relatively old, with high, arched windows that were mostly plain, save for one of stained glass shining down on the nave. Large, dark oak doors stood open to welcome any who wished to step inside.

"You're taking me to a church?" Kaia said. The Garrows had marched her and the other girls to church every Sunday, where as often as not, the vicar would talk about how grateful they should be to receive such charity. This looked grander and older by far, though.

"The vicar is a friend," Pinsley replied.

He led the way inside. The interior had whitewashed walls and wooden pews carved on the ends by a variety of hands. There was no service going on right then, but a man in the dark clothes and dog collar of a vicar was moving around collecting up hymn books. He was in his late thirties, with dark hair and a slightly soft, rounded features obscured slightly by a short beard. He looked nothing like fat Reverend Yale, who led the services at the church nearest the orphanage and tended to forget where he was in his sermons.

"Sebastian," this vicar said as he turned towards them with a warm smile. "How good to see you. And who do you have with you?"

"Lucas," Pinsley said with a nod of recognition. "Sorry, Reverend Faulkner. This is Kaia. She is helping me with an investigation." Kaia heard him sigh. "Lucas, I need a favor. I need somewhere for Kaia to stay, just for tonight."

"Of course," the vicar said, and those were two words Kaia hadn't been expecting. She'd been expecting the inspector to have to argue to get anyone to take on a burden like her.

The vicar nodded to himself. "I'm sure Lottie will be glad of the company in the vicarage. She gets rather bored with just her big brother around to talk to. Although I feel I must point out that if you actually stayed back home, rather than at that club of yours..."

"You know why I do not," Pinsley said. "Besides, it still would not be seemly. Here, at least there is your sister as a responsible chaperone."

"Lottie is going to *love* the idea of being called responsible," Lucas said. He turned his attention to Kaia. "Forgive me, Kaia. I'm ignoring you. Please, come with me."

That was bizarre, being treated as if she mattered. Kaia wasn't sure if the vicar meant it seriously or not. He led the way through the church, out through a door leading to the churchyard. A house sat at the far end, which seemed small and cozy-looking by the standards of some of the townhouses surrounding it, with a dark slate roof, white painted walls and green stained window frames. Roses climbed up the walls, apparently in defiance of the smoke that drifted over from the railway line. To Kaia, it seemed like a country cottage set in the midst of the city. It was the sort of place she couldn't have imagined back in the orphanage.

A woman opened the door as they approached. Her features were shaper than her brother's although there was still the same sense of being about to break into a smile at any moment. She was perhaps a year or two younger than him, as well. She had large eyes and dark, curling hair beneath a bonnet. She wore a tightly cinched dress that seemed like a cascade of colors, each falling over the next.

"Who is this, Lucas? Sebastian?"

"Kaia will be staying with us tonight, Lottie," Lucas said.

"Wonderful," the woman replied, just like that, and again, the kindness of it was almost too much. She held out a hand towards Kaia. "Come with me, dear, and we'll get your room ready. You can have the spare room. Lucas mostly likes to sleep in the vestry, but I'll be around if you need me."

Kaia took her hand and found herself swept along into a home that was all odd angles. There were canvasses set up on easels here and there, while small sculptures and pots stood on every surface. The wall seemed to be in the midst of being repainted a deep blue.

"I see you're feeling inspired again, Lottie," Inspector Pinsley said.

"I've been reading William Morris' thoughts on the use of colors taken from nature," Lottie replied. "But enough of that, we need to get *you* set up, Kaia."

She led the way upstairs, to a room that had a bed at one end on a large rug, a wardrobe set in one corner, and a chest of drawers. There were boxes of what seemed to be more art supplies abandoned around the room. A window looked out towards the church.

"It's rather a mess, I'm afraid," Lottie said. "But I hope it will do for tonight once we dig out some blankets."

It was more space than Kaia had ever had to herself in her life. More than that, it had a door. One that she could shut if she wanted. That meant… it meant more to Kaia than she could put into words. She felt as if she might cry.

"Now, if you're hungry, I'm sure we have something in the pantry," Lottie said. She took Kaia's hand again, leading her back downstairs, to where Inspector Pinsley and Reverend Painton(Faulkner?) were waiting. "Will you be staying for supper, Sebastian?"

"I should get back," the inspector said. He turned to Kaia. "I will see you in the morning. I am trusting you, Kaia."

"I know," Kaia said. "I… I'll be here. Thank you, for all of this. It means so much."

The inspector looked as if he might say something, but mostly he just looked a little embarrassed as he started to walk out.

"Just see that you're here," he said. "I will find you if you run."

CHAPTER THIRTEEN

Kaia knew that the sensible thing to do would be to run. She lay awake, contemplating that, and what it would mean.

Reverend Faulkner and Lottie had been kind, but they were only doing this as a favor to the inspector. Kaia imagined that they would hand her over if he asked, without a second thought. If she left now, she could be across London before morning. She could slip onto a barge and ride the Thames as far as Oxford, or try her original plan of a train out of the city. With the line from Euston so close by, it wouldn't be hard. Lottie was asleep, so sneaking out of the vicarage would be straightforward enough. The church would be easy enough to avoid, and there would undoubtedly be trains from the earliest hours, taking people and goods out into the rest of England.

Kaia wasn't sure what stopped her from actually doing it. Not the inspector's threat. She had no doubt that he meant it, but his reach only extended to London, not to the rest of the country. If anything, the threat of being caught and transported to Australia was a good reason *to* run.

Yet if she ran, she wouldn't find out what was happening. She wouldn't find out what the mark on her arm meant, or why she had such feelings of darkness and dread around places like Bedlam. She would never know who had killed Tabitha Greene, or why, and even though Kaia didn't know the dead woman, she found that it mattered whether she knew or not.

Then there was the fact that she'd made a promise to Pinsley. His threat might not matter, but her word did, at least when it came to him. He was dismissive, abrasive, so sure that his way was the only right one, but he'd also found her this place, and he'd listened to her, back in the carriage. That small act meant more to her than Kaia could imagine. Kaia found herself appreciating him and what he'd done, just a little, although she would never, ever, tell him that.

If she didn't want to run, that left trying to sleep again. Kaia settled back among the covers. She still found herself thing about too many other things. There was the mystery itself, and that was complicated enough, but there were plenty of other things too. There were the strange feelings she'd been having.

Then there was the question of her past. Most days, Kaia pushed away those kinds of thoughts, because they only made the reality around her seem more bleak. Without answers, it was only a kind of pain, asking herself who her parents might have been, trying to imagine what their lives might have been.

Now, though, she imagined them a hundred different ways. Kaia imagined them as simple people, in one of the cities of England, or maybe even further off, in one of the great cities of the wider Empire. Her name was unusual enough by the standards of London, so maybe they *were* from somewhere else.

She imagined them as something more dashing, maybe antiquarians seeking out discoveries among the pyramids of Egypt, or a military officer and his wife, off fighting battles around the world. She imagined them as Roma, rolling along in wheeled wagons, and as nobles fleeing France after the most recent rounds of revolution. She even, briefly, imagined them as some minor royalty, in Eastern Europe, or perhaps one of the multitudes of small states in Italy who might come back for her and take her away to live in a castle.

Somewhere in all of it, Kaia managed to drift into sleep. She slept, and she dreamed. For a brief while, the dreams were simply a continuation of the things she'd been imagining while she was awake, so that she was living lives she'd never had, far away from the filth and smoke of London.

Then something shifted in her dreams. Kaia felt it change subtly at first, with a kind of wrongness that she didn't understand. It felt as if her dreams were not her own, as if she were looking through other eyes, seeing out over the city, and the world.

She saw the streets of London, with their gas lamps and their mists. She saw flickers of other places, cities and open spaces, villages and people living out in wild places. There were people speaking in languages she didn't understand, wearing clothes that would have seemed utterly strange in the middle of London. It should have seemed wondrous, to be able to see so much.

Instead, the sense that something was wrong continued. It took Kaia a moment to realize what the problem was. It was the shadows; something was wrong with the shadows. They flickered where they shouldn't have. They twisted and shifted against the surfaces they sat on, but there was no object there to affect the light in front of them. She saw people moving through crowds, and it seemed that there was something wrong with their shadows too. They moved with them as they walked, but it seemed to Kaia that they didn't just move in the ways the people moved. Instead, they shifted like independent things, moving as if they were staring in Kaia's direction.

Whatever part of her was dreaming fled from that look, and now she was back in London, although how she knew that, she wasn't sure. The walls on either side of her could have been anywhere, yet there was something about the grime of them that suggested London. Kaia saw posters for tonics and shows plastered to walls, confirming it, but right then she wasn't concentrating on those. She was too busy watching the shadow that slid along the wall like a living thing.

In her dream, Kaia followed it, pacing after it like a big game hunter tracking her quarry on foot. She turned a corner, and now she knew where she was, because St Michael's Church stood ahead of her, the stained glass exactly the way it had been when she and Inspector Pinsley had first arrived at it.

Kaia couldn't see the shadow now, but she could still feel the sense that something was utterly wrong. She could feel that wrongness coming from the church, pushing at her as if urging her to run away. Something was happening there, and whatever it was, it was terrifying, in a presence that seemed to envelop everything she was, making it hard to breathe, making it hard to think…

Kaia woke up, gasping, and for a few seconds she had no idea where she was. She could have been back in the orphanage then, trying not to cry out in sudden terror because of the trouble it would cause if Mrs. Garrow heard someone not being quiet enough. She found herself lying in her nightdress, tangled in her blankets so that she had to struggle free of them before she was able to get up.

Kaia did so, taking deep breaths and trying to tell herself to stay calm. It had just been a dream, and there was nothing to worry about. It certainly wasn't worth waking up Lottie for. Better to just calm down and go back to sleep. Still, Kaia couldn't shake the feeling that something was wrong, so she moved over to the window for a moment or two, pulling aside the curtain and looking out towards the spot where the church stood just across the yard.

There was a light inside, glowing through the stained glass. That was probably nothing, when Reverend Faulkner slept in the vestry, but every instinct Kaia had told her that something was wrong, and it took an effort not to run across there to find out.

She heard something, although at this distance it was hard to tell exactly what. It might have been a man's voice, crying out in anger, or in fear, but Kaia couldn't tell for sure. Still, it was enough to prompt her into movement. She dressed as quickly as she could, pulling on her dress and fastening the buttons of her boots.

Kaia crept out of her room on tiptoes. She supposed that she ought to wake up Lottie and tell her about her concerns, but right then she wasn't sure what she would say. It was better to be certain about what was happening, rather than waking the vicar's sister up just for a bad dream.

Kaia padded downstairs, and made her way towards the door, trying to remember where the cluttered art supplies of the cottage were in the dark. She misjudged it, though, and found her elbow brushing against one of the easels. She felt a canvas start to fall, and grabbed for it, terrified about the trouble it might cause if the whole thing went clattering to the ground.

Kaia was fast enough to catch it, just, and she eased it back into place. She set it upright and moved away from it as carefully as she could. She made her way to the front door, found it locked, and then had to feel around until she found a set of keys resting on a hook. Working purely by touch, Kaia sorted through the keys, trying them in the lock one after another until she managed to open it with a click.

The sense that something awful was happening was growing in her by the second. Kaia couldn't explain it, and wasn't even sure that anything was really happening in the church, but she inched the door open anyway. She slipped out into the cold of the February night, and then closed the door as softly as she could.

The light was still coming from the church. As quietly as she could, holding the keys still so that they wouldn't make a sound, Kaia made her way towards its door, determined to find out what was happening there that made the sense of wrongness fill her so utterly.

CHAPTER FOURTEEN

Kaia stepped into the church, and it was almost as cold inside as out. The sense of wrongness grew with every pace she took forward, into the north transept of St Michael's, building into something more. She wanted to run away. She wanted to get out of there, but she didn't run. Instead, Kaia used that sense of wrongness the way a sailor might have used a compass, pulling her forward inexorably.

It helped that doing so also involved taking her towards the part of the church that was lit. That light was a beacon drawing her forward, past the door to the vestry, and on towards the altar.

Kaia could see now that the light was coming from candles set all around the church, burning brightly against the darkness. There were more there than Kaia had ever seen at once, rendering the church almost as bright as daylight within. Even so, shadows danced in the corners of the building, shifting with the flickering of the flames.

Kaia gasped at the sight of two figures struggling in the midst of that brightness. Reverend Faulkner was one of them, but it was hard to tell anything about the other, because he was wearing dark, shapeless clothes, with a scarf wrapped around the lower part of his face and a dark, short hat covering the upper part.

Even as Kaia watched, he bore the vicar down to the ground, slamming him into a spot where the light stone of the floor gave way to a darker slab laid in memory of some benefactor or other. Kaia could only watch in terror as the attacker held Reverend Faulkner there in spite of his attempts to buck his way clear. The man in black knelt, straddling the vicar's chest, and his gloved hands went down to wrap around Reverend Faulkner's throat. Kaia heard him gurgle and gasp as the other man started to choke the life out of him.

She stood there, not knowing what to do. She was not large or strong, and she had no weapon that might have helped her fend off a man like this. She didn't even know anything about fighting, because Mrs. Garrow had been swift to punish such unladylike behavior with her cane whenever two girls came to blows. There was no obvious way to help directly.

So what should she do? She couldn't run, not when that would leave the vicar at the mercy of the man who was trying to kill him. She could cry for help, but what guarantee was there that anyone would hear her? Almost involuntarily, Kaia took a step forward. Even if she didn't know anything about fighting, she could at least push this man off Reverend Faulkner.

Running up to him, Kaia pushed the man as hard as she could, shoving him back off the vicar's chest. The attacker seemed to twist as he tumbled off, coming up to his feet and looking down at Kaia through the lenses of smoked glass spectacles that hid his eyes.

Even so, Kaia could sense a kind of hatred there that she'd never encountered before in her life. It was a hatred of everything she was, every instant of her existence. It was something that felt beyond anything human. That sense of wrongness she'd been feeling since she woke up was amplified a thousand-fold looking into the dark glass in front of those eyes.

"Kaia," Reverend Faulkner rasped, "run. Save yourself."

Kaia wished that she could take his advice, but her feet felt like lead then. She was absolutely terrified, but she couldn't move, trapped like a hare in a poacher's lamp glow. She couldn't even back away as the figure opposite her took a step straight towards her, the feeling of malevolence building until it was almost overwhelming.

Something rose within her to match that feeling. The sensation was of being filled as if she might burst with something that burned within her, something that Kaia didn't understand, but which felt as if it might consume her if she didn't find a way to let it out. It hurt, and she fell to her knees with that pain, clutching her head as it felt as if it might explode. It was as if she were a volcano waiting to erupt, filled with more pressure and fire than she could even begin to handle.

Kaia did the only thing she could do in that moment, and screamed.

It was the loudest sound that had ever come from her, and probably the loudest sound she had ever heard. It was hard to believe that it was her own voice issuing the sound, which rattled out around the church, seeming to fill it the way it had filled her before. The man in black stumbled back, his hands over his ears as if he might shut out the sound.

Still, the scream continued. It seemed to have a life of its own now, tearing from Kaia's throat with a force she couldn't begin to believe. Reverend Faulkner was clutching a cross, his lips moving in a prayer that Kaia couldn't hear over the sound that issued forth from her, and still the power built.

She flinched as glass broke around her. The great stained glass window in the nave exploded, sending showers of glass out towards the street. The leaded panes of the other windows in the church broke an instant later, breaking into tiny fragments that flew out as if they had been blasted by a hurricane.

Then, snatched at by the same impossible force, every candle in the church went out.

As the echoes of the scream faded, Kaia heard movement in the dark, and she was terrified that the man in black might be lunging at her even as she knelt there. She felt something pass by her, far closer than she wanted. More movement came nearby, far too close, something scrabbling in the dark…

Then Reverend Faulkner used one of the matches he was fumbling with to re-light the first of the candles, starting to illuminate the interior of St Michael's again, little by little. He staggered between the candles, his hands shaking as he used one to light the next, but he didn't stop until a soft glow suffused the church.

Kaia found herself feeling exhausted, so that she needed Reverend Faulkner's help to stand and move to one of the pews. It felt as if she'd put everything she had into that scream, so that right now, there was nothing left of her. The reverend looked almost as worn out. He seemed shaken by the attack, and Kaia could see the bruises blossoming on his neck.

There was no sign of the man who had attacked the vicar. He was gone, presumably out through the open main door of the church. Kaia was still contemplating that when Lottie ran in, wearing her night things, and carrying what appeared to be an overly large rifle.

"Is everything all right?" Lottie asked as she strode in. "That *sound*."

Kaia could only laugh at the sight of her there like that, and she was grateful for that laughter. It seemed to cut into the terror and the exhaustion of the last few minutes, letting her start to breathe normally again.

"Lottie, you aren't dressed," Reverend Faulkner said, in a faintly weary tone that suggested that he was doing all of this automatically, because the alternative was thinking too hard about what had just happened.

"Well, if you were in trouble, would you really want to be waiting for me to finish tying the stays of my corset before I came to help?"

"And the elephant gun? Really?"

"Well, *I* didn't know what was going on," Lottie said. She sighed. "What *was* happening, Lucas?"

"I'll explain shortly," Reverend Faulkner said. "For now, I think I should speak with Kaia. Why don't you go and fetch us all some tea? Possibly putting away the gun and putting on a dress while you do so?"

"Tea?" Lottie said, as she turned to leave. "I was thinking brandy."

Reverend Faulkner sat down beside Kaia. She wasn't sure what to say right then, or even what to think.

"Where did your sister get a gun like that?" she asked, because it was easier than asking about the impossibility of what had just happened to her.

"She picked it up on the grand tour, I believe," Reverend Faulkner said. His voice still didn't seem quite as steady as it had been before. "Suffice it to say that my sister has lived an… interesting life. I am more interested in what you just managed to do, Kaia."

"I'm sorry," Kaia said, automatically. Would they throw her out for this? Was she going to have to run after all?

Reverend Faulkner raised an eyebrow. "You're apologizing for saving my life?"

"For breaking all of your windows," Kaia said, even though she was still having a hard time connecting anything she might be able to do to the destruction around the church. Mrs. Garrow would already have been screaming at her for doing so much damage.

"I am more interested in *how* you managed to do that," Reverend Faulkner said.

"I don't know," Kaia said. "I… it was like there was a power inside me, and it just burst out. I couldn't control it."

"And why were you here in the church at all, Kaia?" Reverend Faulkner said. "How did you know to come here and help me?"

"I…" Kaia was going to tell him that she'd seen the lights in the church and heard him cry out, but she stopped short. "I had a dream. I saw… there was a shadow." Something occurred to her. "Why did you light so many candles?"

Reverend Faulkner sat there for a second, clasping his hands around the cross he held until his knuckles tightened. Kaia had the sense that he was trying to determine how much to tell her, or perhaps how to say any of it in a way that made sense.

"There is more to this world than we think, Kaia. There is a lot of darkness in it. People react to that in different ways, we seek answers in different ways. Sebastian deals with it through reason. I have my faith. My sister... well, it is hard to tell with her. Sometimes though, we must accept that there are things beyond what we know. Things that are unseen. Sometimes, the most we can do is light candles to drive away the dark."

"Is that what you were doing?" Kaia asked.

"You have a much greater light inside you, Kaia," Reverend Faulkner said. "The fact that you were able to do something like this is... well, it is incredible. It is something that makes you very special."

Special? No one had ever called Kaia special before. They had certainly never talked about her having a light within her.

"You could potentially do a lot of good," Reverend Faulkner said. "But you must also be careful, Kaia."

"Careful?"

"Light attracts darkness," the vicar said, and now he looked round as if checking for danger. "The brighter the light, the further away things can see it that might want to snuff your light out forever."

That was a thought that frightened Kaia. "You think that the man tonight was here because of me?"

"I don't know," Reverend Faulkner said. He sounded as if he didn't like not knowing. "But I will keep your secret until you are ready to tell others, and we will do everything we can to keep you safe."

That meant more than Kaia could say, although, looking around at the destruction in the church, it was hard for her to imagine that she was safe at all. Someone was out there, filled with a darkness she couldn't name, and she'd seen in one look that the darkness wanted her dead.

Kaia was sure that this had something to do with Tabitha Greene's death. She wasn't sure what, or how she was so certain, but this was a part of it. Find her killer, and she would find the man who had attacked them tonight.

CHAPTER FIFTEEN

Inspector Pinsley slept at his club that night, as he did most nights these days. The Raventrop wasn't quite in the league of those clubs that catered to the finest gentlemen, but it was still a place for respectable officers and barristers, even the occasional member of parliament. The food was simple and solid, the conversation in the armchairs there enlightening, and the watered whiskey very nearly the finest.

The rooms were meant to be for those who overindulged to sleep things off without a scandal, but Pinsley had been staying there for months now. Tonight, he lay staring at the ceiling, hunting for sleep and unable to find it. That was nothing new, either.

Eventually, his eyes fluttered closed, but that only brought the sight of Catherine to him in his dreams. She was walking beside him in a park, the paleness of her dress billowing around her in the wind. The same wind caught her bonnet, taking it from her head and setting it soaring ahead of her. Her dark hair streamed behind her as she laughed and ran, so that he had to chase after both her and the bonnet.

Pinsley remembered this day. He'd caught up to her just as she reached the hat and managed to snatch it first, holding it away from her until she'd kissed him most scandalously to distract him and snatch it back.

That wasn't what happened in the dream, though. In that, he found himself stuck behind Catherine, chasing as hard as he could but still unable to catch up to her. He could feel a sense of dread growing in his chest, and he knew what he would see next, however much he tried to stop it, to look away, to do *anything* but see this moment…

He was looking down at his wife's body, lying there bloodied and beaten in their home. There was blood over everything, forming dark stains across the carpets and spattering the walls. There were cuts over her flesh that had to have been made by a knife, while there were bruises on her throat from strangling hands. The sheer horror of it was too much for Pinsley, and he fell to his knees beside her, unable to look away, however much he wanted to.

Now, though, she was receding from him again, slipping away, no matter how desperately he tried to keep hold of her...

Pinsley woke, gasping and managing not to cry out. Not that it would have mattered. The Raventrop had more than its share of officers who had seen too much in the war. If they thought that his demons came from the same place, Pinsley wasn't going to enlighten them.

He could feel the wetness of tears on his cheeks, and wiped them away quickly. He knew that it was just a dream, but it was as if his heart broke all over again each time he woke up from it, as if Catherine died in front of him, over and over.

Inevitably, after thinking of Catherine, his thoughts went to Olivia. How many times had he tried to find his daughter now? No matter how hard he'd tried, though, she was gone, lost in the depths of London, or gone somewhere beyond it. He knew that he'd been too caught up in his grief to see her pain after her mother's death, or the things she was doing to ease it. Even when she'd disappeared, he'd been too slow to act, and now Olivia was gone.

Pinsley rose, and poured himself a watered whiskey from the decanter he kept at the bedside. It stilled his nerves a little, but not enough. He took out his metronome, winding it and setting it in motion. The tick of it helped to bring his thoughts back to order, as it always did.

He found those thoughts moving to Kaia, and he found it odd that they should move so swiftly from his daughter to her. Strictly speaking, he knew that he should have taken her back to the station for the night. Leaving her with Lucas and Lottie was an invitation for her to run. It was what he would have done in her place.

He should have taken her to the station. In fact, he should probably have left her there, for the law to take its course. If there had been anything to gain by bringing her along with him, that moment had passed now. Logic, and the requirements of his position, dictated that he should put her back where he had found her. He owed her a word about her helpfulness to a magistrate, but no more than that.

So why hadn't he done any of that? Part of it was that she was the same age his daughter would be now, but that wasn't all of it. More of it was that, whenever he looked at her, Pinsley couldn't help the feeling that there was far more going on behind her eyes. There were things that Kaia wasn't saying, perhaps that she was afraid to say. As much as he was committed to reason, something far less reasonable told Pinsley that those things might be the key to all of this.

Thoughts of Olivia were uncomfortable, though. What if he managed to drive Kaia away the way he'd driven off his daughter? What if he went back to the church and found her gone?

Rising quickly, Pinsley hurried from his club. He needed to get back to Kaia before it was too late.

*

Pinsley sat in his cab, wishing that the horses would go faster, and cursing himself for his foolishness. He knew he was probably going to arrive at St Michael's Church only to find her gone. How was he going to explain that to his superiors? Probably Superintendent Hutton would rub his hands with glee at Pinsley making such an error.

The cab rounded the last corner before the church, and Pinsley found himself staring at it in shock. Glass littered the churchyard around it, so that it seemed that every window in it had been destroyed. Pinsley alighted from the cab, walking over and trying to make some sense of it. It looked as if the glass had been broken from the inside, but beyond that, there was nothing to tell him what had happened.

He walked swiftly around to the vicarage, and was relieved to see that at least it hadn't been damaged in the same way as the church. He knocked, and didn't have to wait more than a minute before Lucas opened the door.

"Is Kaia here?" Pinsley asked, before the vicar could even say good morning. That was the most vital question of all of them, perhaps the one on which Pinsley's future as a police inspector depended.

"Yes, of course she is," Lucas said. "She is just sitting down to breakfast with us. Will you join us, Sebastian?"

Relief flooded through Pinsley.

"I… that would be good," Pinsley admitted. He looked the vicar over. "What happened to your neck, Lucas? Why is it bruised?" He put that fact together with the damage to the church. "Did something happen last night that I should be aware of?"

"Come through to breakfast, and I shall explain," Lucas said. "But we'd best be quick. I will need to spend the morning organizing a subscription to pay for replacement glass, and I still have services to give today. Three funerals and a wedding. It seems that as ever in London, the sad threatens to outweigh the happy."

"I'm sure you'll find a way to work it into your services," Pinsley said, although not harshly.

"All life is inspiration," Lucas agreed.

Lucas led the way through the vicarage to the dining room, where Pinsley had his next big surprise of the day. Seated at a small, circular dining table were Lottie, dressed in her usual odd assortment of colors, and Kaia, who…

Only Pinsley's iron self-control kept him from staring open mouthed. She didn't look like the same girl. The girl Pinsley had plucked from the cells had been wearing a dirty dress, ripped in her scuffle with the constables. She had been dirt stained as well, even her brief time on London's streets starting to leave its mark.

Now, she was scrubbed clean, and wearing a lightly hooped lilac dress over the usual layers of underskirts. A dark corset that was probably one of Lottie's spares cinched her waist enough to provide support, and she wore a broad brimmed hat that was probably one of Lottie's art projects, judging by the trio of feathers poking from a hand-woven band around it. A coat and scarf hung on the back of her chair, and Pinsley found himself feeling guilty for just how much of London he'd dragged her across in February without either.

"Do you like it?" Kaia asked. "Lottie found some of her old things."

"They're very nice," Pinsley said, hiding his surprise at all this as best he could. Lucas was already setting a place for him at the breakfast table, setting out a plate of smoked kippers and eggs. He sat and ate gratefully. Still, he couldn't ignore what he'd seen as he walked past the church. "Tell me, what happened here last night?"

He could see the tension in all three of them in the moments before Lucas answered him.

"There was an intruder," he said. "He came into the church and started breaking all of the windows. I remonstrated with him and he attacked me. Kaia heard me call out and came to my aid, pushing him from me. He ran off. Probably he saw that Lottie was coming with a gun."

Pinsley took all that in, trying to make some sense of it.

"Were you hurt, Kaia?" he asked. He was more worried about that than he'd thought he might be.

"No, I'm fine," she said. She looked away as she said it, and Pinsley was sure that there was something about this that she wasn't telling him.

"And did you see the man who came into the church? Could you describe him?"

79

She shook her head. "He was wearing all black, and he had his face covered."

"Yes, but there has to be more to it than that," Pinsley began.

"Tell me, Sebastian," Lottie said, slightly too loudly. "Do you think the Whigs are likely to fall from government? Will Lillywhite score many runs this season, do you think? Will we add to Hong Kong when this whole wretched business in China is done?"

"Subtle, Lottie," Pinsley said, although by her standards it probably counted as exactly that.

"I'm merely reminding you that the breakfast table isn't the best place for an interrogation, Sebastian," she replied. "Kaia has told you what she knows, and last night was quite distressing enough for her."

It was obvious that there was something they weren't telling him. It seemed like too much of a coincidence that a man like that should have come into the church immediately after Pinsley had left Kaia there. If it had been anyone else there, Pinsley would have pressed the point, but Lottie and Lucas were his closest remaining friends, and he wasn't about to risk that.

Besides, there were bigger mysteries to be solved, and the only way they were likely to solve them was to get out into the city and ask questions.

"Are you ready to go?" Pinsley asked Kaia when they were finished eating.

She nodded. "Where are we going?"

"I've been thinking about what you said," he said. "And I want to find whoever sent Tabitha Greene to Bedlam."

CHAPTER SIXTEEN

As they went out onto the streets of London, Kaia wasn't sure if she should tell the inspector the truth of what had happened last night. Reverend Faulkner had insisted that she shouldn't, and her instincts said that it made her sound dangerously mad, but still, a part of her *wanted* to trust Inspector Pinsley.

For now, though, she followed in his wake. They were walking this morning, at a brisk pace that meant Kaia occasionally had to run a few steps to keep up. She was determined to not just be a silent face beside Pinsley today though, as she had been for so much of their trip to Bedlam. She was determined to help more than that.

"Where are we going today?" she asked, as they made their way south, along streets that were just starting to fill up with people and horses. They were keeping Regent's Park on their right, across the railway lines. The day was colder than yesterday, but now Kaia was wrapped up warm in her borrowed coat and scarf.

"Your suggestion that Tabitha Greene might have been put in Bedlam precisely so that she could be killed bears investigation," Pinsley said. "According to the records in Bedlam, the name of the doctor who committed her was de Vere, but there was no address given for his practice."

"You remember that just from looking through the records?" Kaia asked, impressed.

"Remembering is easy," Pinsley replied. "Making sense of it all, or seeing the importance of things, is another matter."

"So, why are we walking?" Kaia asked, as they kept going. A train steamed past them in a burst of noise and smoke that briefly left Kaia coughing.

"Are you afraid of getting your new dress dirty?" Pinsley asked her, with a faint smile.

"No," Kaia replied. Did he think that she would care more about a new dress than anything else? "I just know that you don't do anything without a reason, and I want to know what the next thing is in our investigation."

"So it's our investigation now?" Pinsley asked.

Kaia nodded. "I want answers as badly as you do."

She probably wanted them *more* than he, after what had happened last night. Tabitha Greene and what had happened to her held the key to all of it, Kaia was sure of that much.

"We're walking so that we can ask questions," Pinsley said. He stopped by the stall of a whelk seller, lowering his voice. The man there shook his head, and Pinsley kept walking.

"So when you want to know things, you ask random hawkers out on the street?" Kaia asked.

"There's nothing random about it. Albert there has stood in the same spot for going on ten years. He sees who goes past, although I think we will have to talk to some of my people closer to where Tabitha lived, before we start to find out more about her and her life."

"Your people?" Kaia said. It made it sound as if the inspector had some vast network of spies working for him.

"I've made it my business to find those who know what is happening in London," Pinsley said. "On both sides of the law. Now, this way. Tabitha's last listed address was in Bloomsbury."

To Kaia, that was another part of London, like Marylebone or Westminster that almost seemed like some made-up, far-off land compared to the dingy conditions of the orphanage and its surrounds. Yet at the side of the inspector, she found herself walking down towards it, so that the great neoclassical edifice of the British Museum and the University of London stood in the distance.

They turned away from those briefly, though, and instead, they headed in a different direction. Kaia didn't understand it until she saw the name of the street they'd come to: Harley Street.

"At least twenty doctors have their offices here," Inspector Pinsley said. "A woman living where Tabitha Greene did might well have a doctor here. To go further would be impractical."

"Would the doctor be *her* doctor though?" Kaia asked. "If someone else were having her committed so that she could be murdered, wouldn't they be the one choosing the doctor involved?"

"That is a valid point," the inspector said. "Still, I think they would choose someone associated with Miss Greene, or with ready access to her. We should at least check to see if Doctor de Vere has set up his practice here."

They made their way along the tall townhouses, with Kaia checking the names on the brass nameplates as they went.

"Johnson…" She dodged out of the way of a servant sweeping the step and ran on to the next house. "Naismith…" The inspector was falling a little behind now, but there was something fun about running ahead, trying to find their target before he did. Besides, Kaia needed answers at least as badly as he did. "de Vere. This is the one!"

She waited there while the inspector rang the bell. A servant, a young woman who was obviously there to clean and cook, came to greet them, and Inspector Pinsley handed over his card.

"We wish to see Doctor de Vere. It is in relation to a former patient of his."

"I'm afraid the doctor is not at home at the moment. He is out on a house call, and it is hard to say when he might be back. If you would care to wait…"

"We'll return later," Pinsley promised, gesturing for Kaia to move away from the door. The servant shut it, and the two of them started the walk back up the street.

"So we know where the doctor is," Kaia said. "But we can't speak to him. What now?"

"Now, we go and find out more while we wait," the inspector said. He pointed. "The market is just this way."

*

Pinsley watched Kaia's expression of astonishment as they walked around Bloomsbury, as if she couldn't believe that a place like this really existed. She gave the British Museum a hungry look, as if she would have liked nothing more than to spend the rest of the day looking around it.

"So that holds objects from all around the world?" Kaia said.

"From all the furthest outposts of the British Empire," Pinsley agreed. "The reading room there opened last year. They say there's space to house a million books."

"A million?" Kaia looked at him as if she couldn't believe that there were that many books in existence.

Pinsley had his own memories when it came to the museum. He'd taken his daughter there once, and she'd stared, fascinated, at the objects on display. This was no time to revisit those memories, though, because they had work to do.

"We won't find answers in there today," he said. He nodded in the direction of Bloomsbury Market instead. "That's where we'll learn what we need."

They headed down among the barrows and the market stalls. Where some markets in London specialized in fish or vegetables, flowers or old goods, this market was more general, so that a stall selling bolts of cloth might be next to one selling potatoes, or sharpening knives.

Pinsley knew the patterns of the place as well as he knew the rest of London. He stopped at a spot where a couple of young men were eyeing the crowd, obviously trying to size it up for marks.

"Jim Matthews, Archie Matthews, I see you," he said. He grabbed the shoulder of the nearest one as he saw the young man tense. "No, don't run, Jim. I've things I need to ask, first."

Kaia stood to one side, looking on.

"We don't know anything," the one under Pinsley's grip complained. "We haven't done anything."

"There's no point in lying. We both know that you two are the best when it comes to lifting wallets," Pinsley said. "The only reason I haven't arrested you already is because I'm meant to deal with more serious crimes, and because you know everyone in this city. So make yourselves useful, tell me something I want to know, and you can be on your way."

"Who's the girl?" Jim asked, staring over at Kaia.

"None of your concern," Pinsley said, shaking him. It was important not to get Kaia mixed up with the likes of these petty cutpurses. It didn't help that she seemed to be watching them as carefully as Pinsley might have, as if trying to discern the truth by watching them.

"What do you want to know, copper?" Archie asked.

"I want to know what you can tell me about two people who live near here. One's a young woman who was taken off to Bedlam not long ago, by the name of Tabitha Greene. The other's a doctor, called de Vere."

"We don't exactly hang out with the posh folk," Jim complained.

"They're lying, aren't they?" Kaia said. "That one twitches when he's trying to hide something."

Pinsley was impressed. "Not bad." He returned his attention to Jim. "You watch them every day while you're trying to work out what to lift, and from whom. Last chance, or I'm arresting the pair of you."

"All right, all right!" Jim said. "I *think* I know the woman you mean. Used to buy her hats at one of the milliners' stalls there. Same time she'd come by every market day, then just gone. Never could get close enough to lift anything from her. The doctor, well, there's a doctor with a French name comes over here. Looking plush the last little while."

"You'll need to give me more than that," Pinsley said in a warning tone.

"They say he goes up to Soho sometimes, but that's all we know, I swear," Archie said.

Pinsley shoved Jim away from him, and the two took that as their cue to run. He let them.

"They didn't tell us much," Kaia said.

"Honestly, I'm astonished that they told us that much," Pinsley said. "People are far too often invisible to one another."

"So," Kaia said, "are we going to talk to this hat seller?"

Pinsley nodded. "She may be able to tell us something about Tabitha."

They went over to a stall where a delicate woman in her thirties was stitching the last beads to a fascinator.

"Here to get something for your daughter?" she asked, as they approached. "That's a lovely hat she has already, but I'm sure we can find something to add to it."

Pinsley froze at the word "daughter," unable to even take out his warrant card. It hadn't occurred to him that it might be the way someone might see Kaia. The thought of it made a tangle of memories of Oliva come to mind, with her wandering through markets, picking out what she wanted.

Pinsley knew that he should be saying something, trying to get information. Thankfully, Kaia was already talking.

"That's right," she said. "A friend of the family recommended you. Tabitha Greene?"

"Tabitha?" the stallholder's expression grew sadder for a moment. "Such a pity what happened to her. She was always so bright and happy, and… well, maybe she was always a little eccentric, but to be shut away like that, and her own brother doing it?"

"Her brother?" Pinsley said, unable to stop himself.

"Still," the stallholder said, and Pinsley got the impression that any chance she might say more was gone, "we probably shouldn't talk about such things. Now, do you see anything you like?"

Kaia browsed over the stall for a minute or two, until Pinsley felt obliged to purchase a length of beading for the brim of her hat just so it wouldn't look suspicious. He looked over at her as they walked away.

"You lie suspiciously well," he said.

"It seemed easier than trying to bully her into talking like the others," Kaia said.

"I wasn't just talking about that," Pinsley replied. "I know that you, Lucas, and Lottie aren't telling me the whole story about last night."

"What about the things you aren't telling me?" Kaia countered.

Pinsley stopped short. "What do you mean?"

"Do you think I haven't seen the haunted look that comes over you sometimes? Especially when you look at me. You did it when I was looking at the museum. Who do I remind you of, Inspector?"

A burst of pain flashed through Pinsley, and he recoiled from the thought of being so easy to read. "*That* is a private matter. We will not speak of it again."

"And *you* don't get to know everything about *me*," Kaia shot back.

Pinsley stood there for a moment or two longer, trying to gather himself. He would not stand there in the street and argue with a girl young enough to be… to be his daughter. No, he wouldn't think about that. He wouldn't.

He started walking away from Kaia, just so that she wouldn't see his face.

"Where are we going now?" she asked, hurrying along behind him.

"Tabitha Greene's home," Pinsley said. "Let's see if there is any more light to shed on all this there."

CHAPTER SEVENTEEN

The house was a tall town house, quite close to the museum, and spread over four stories. A series of names and numbers outside suggested that it was divided up into flats. Kaia saw Pinsley frowning at that slightly.

"What is it?" she asked. Kaia wasn't sure what she'd been expecting from Tabitha Greene's home. From the area, she sort of understood that it would be grander than anything she'd known growing up, but still, a part of her couldn't square that with the idea of a woman stuck in Bedlam.

"These are living arrangements I would expect more from a young bachelor," the inspector said. "Living in a flat at the heart of a fashionable part of the city, rather than with her family. It implies something about that relationship, I think. It is an assertion of independence from them, at the very least. But one that was supported, at least in part, or she would not have the means to do this."

"How do we do this?" Kaia asked, looking up at the forbidding dark green of the front door, with a brass knocker shaped like a lion's head. Shouldn't someone who could afford to live *here* be able to afford better than the asylum she'd ended up in?

"Directly," Pinsley said, striding up to the door and rapping the knocker against its plate.

"What if there's no one in?" Kaia started to ask, but even as she did it, an older woman in a dark dress and white apron opened the door. She had white hair curling under her bonnet, and slightly crabbed fingers clutched a broom. Kaia guessed that she was a housekeeper.

"Oh, you startled me," the woman said. "Do forgive me. I'm afraid, if you're here to see any of the residents no one is at home right now."

"This is where Tabitha Greene lived?" Inspector Pinsley asked, in a businesslike tone that seemed to leave no room for polite chattering on the doorstep.

"If you're looking for Miss Greene, I'm sorry, but she is currently away in Harrogate, taking the waters at the spa," the housekeeper said, in a faint Scottish accent.

"A pleasant fiction," Pinsley said. "Who coached you to say that rather than the truth?"

"Sir, I-"

"Until the early hours of yesterday morning, when she was killed by an unknown assailant, Miss Greene was being held in Bedlam."

The housekeeper took a staggering step back. "Killed? What kind of a thing is that to say? Who are you? What are you doing here?"

Kaia saw Pinsley take out his warrant card, holding it up for her to see. The moment he did it, the housekeeper seemed to collapse in on herself, slumping down to the ground with only her broom to hold her up.

Kaia went to her instinctively, helping her back to her feet. The housekeeper was crying now, tears pouring down her face.

"She's really dead?" the housekeeper said. "She's… no, she can't be."

"She is," Pinsley said. "And now I need to find the person who did it. To do that, I need to see where she lived."

"No, she wouldn't have wanted that," the housekeeper said. "And the police can't just go stomping everywhere among her things. No, go away."

"She would want us to catch her killer," Pinsley said.

"No," the housekeeper said.

"Madam, I really must insist," Pinsley replied.

Kaia stepped past him. "You're being too hard on her. You can't just bully people until you get what you want."

He looked a little surprised at her saying that, and perhaps a little ashamed with it. Good. He couldn't make the housekeeper tell him anything. He couldn't make *Kaia* tell him anything. She had to remember that.

"What's your name?" Kaia asked the housekeeper.

"Mrs. Hoyle. Flora Hoyle. This is all such a shock."

"I know," Kaia said, patting her on the shoulder. "Maybe it would be a good idea if we all sat down and had a cup of tea. Perhaps in Miss Greene's rooms? We really *are* trying to help. I'm sure you want whoever did this caught."

Mrs. Hoyle nodded, but then looked over towards where Pinsley stood. "He's not coming in."

"Madam," Pinsley began, "I am a representative of the law."

"You think I don't know the law?" Mrs. Hoyle said. "You can't come in without a warrant from a magistrate, so you're staying where you are. *You* can come in though, dear."

"Madam-" Pinsley began again, and to Kaia's shock, the housekeeper just shut the door in his face.

"I will not abide rudeness," the older woman said. "Come along, dear."

Kaia wasn't sure if she was following the housekeeper, or helping her up the stairs to the top floor, where Mrs. Hoyle unlocked a second door, letting them through into a flat that held a central sitting area, a small kitchen space to one side. A door suggested a bedroom. The furnishings were elegant pale wood and patterned upholstery, with rugs on the floor and books here and there.

It was the sort of space that Kaia could barely have imagined after years in the orphanage. Supposedly, one woman had lived there, but it seemed more like a space for twenty people. To collect herself, she focused on helping the housekeeper.

"You sit down, Mrs. Hoyle," Kaia suggested. "I'll get the tea."

"Oh, Miss Greene wouldn't want that," the housekeeper said. "She doesn't... she *didn't* like guests having to do anything. She was very gracious, even with me, and I'm just the help."

"Her death seems to have affected you a lot," Kaia said, as she sat down on one of the chairs in the living area. Mrs. Hoyle went over to the stove, starting to boil an iron kettle on it.

"She was such a lovely girl," the housekeeper said. "I come round here every other day, when I'm not doing for the house on Grosvenor Street to keep it ready for visitors."

"So this isn't the only house she had?" Kaia asked. She was trying to think what questions the inspector might ask, because she knew that he would want to know everything that transpired here, and she was determined to show that she could pay attention to the details too.

"That her family owns," Mrs. Hoyle corrected her. "Their main estate is out in Surrey, of course. Everyone in Society knows the Greenes. Or knew them, I should say."

That sounded like the sort of thing the inspector would expect her to latch onto.

"Knew them?" Kaia asked.

"It's part of what makes all of this such a tragedy," Mrs. Hoyle explained. She brought over the tea things on a tray. Kaia waited for her to pour. Mrs. Garrow had been very determined that all the girls should learn the correct etiquette. She wasn't going to send them off to a patron without knowing they would be obedient and polite at all times.

"How so?" Kaia asked.

"There was... a fire," Mrs. Hoyle said. "Almost a year ago now, while they were staying up by Loch Lomond over the summer. Her parents both died in that fire."

Kaia tried to imagine the tragedy of that. She knew what it was to grow up without parents, but to have them and then to find them snatched away... in a way, it would be worse. She found herself feeling more and more sympathy for Tabitha Greene. She needed to focus, though. What would Inspector Pinsley ask now?

"Did Tabitha inherit this place from them?" she asked.

"Among other things," Mrs. Hoyle said. "Tabitha's life was..."

When she fell silent, Kaia tried to work out if she should say something. "It's all right, Mrs. Hoyle. Whatever it is, you can say it."

"Her life was not conventional," Mrs. Hoyle said. "She should have been married and settled, with the inheritance passing into the control of her husband, or a trust. Instead, with all this business about shadows and such... how was she ever meant to get a husband, when people thought she was mad? Her parents realized that she would need to be provided for. A young man could go and get a job with one of the banks, or take a commission in the army. A woman doesn't have that range of choices. With enough wealth, though, and in the artistic sets around here, she would merely be thought eccentric."

Kaia tried to take that in. "So how much did they leave her?"

"Several properties," Mrs. Hoyle said. "And some money. Although with her being committed, I think things have become... complicated in probate. I'm sorry, dear, I'm babbling."

"That's all right, Mrs. Hoyle," Kaia said. "I know it's a lot to ask, but may I take a look through Tabitha's things? Did she keep a journal? I need to see if I can find out if she was in touch with anyone, or had any enemies, anything like that."

She *didn't* say that she was hoping for something about shadows, something that would help her to understand all of this.

"I'm sorry, dear," Mrs. Hoyle said. "You can look if you want, but I think her doctor took anything like that."

"Doctor de Vere?"

"That's right, dear. He said it would help to understand her condition better."

Kaia looked anyway. Eventually, though, she had to give up. There really wasn't anything left that might tell her what Tabitha had been thinking. She didn't feel like much of a detective. She just had to hope that what she *had* found would be of some use.

*

When Kaia went downstairs, Inspector Pinsley was standing in exactly the same spot he'd been in when she'd gone up. He stood like a soldier at attention, unmoving as his eyes scanned the street beyond. Even so, he turned as Kaia approached, looking at her with a mixture of impatience and curiosity, clearly not happy at being left on the doorstep, and yet probably hoping it was worth it.

"Well?" he asked.

"I'm not sure," Kaia replied.

"I should have insisted on coming up with you," Pinsley said.

"She wouldn't have let you," Kaia said. "Not after you upset her."

Pinsley nodded. "You're right. Walk with me a moment?"

He led the way out onto the street, and Kaia walked with him.

"What did she say while you were up there?" the inspector asked.

Kaia did her best to recall it. "She said that Tabitha's parents died, and that she stood to inherit a lot of money. There's an estate out in Surrey. She said that Tabitha being put in Bedlam changed all that, that the will was… stuck in probate."

"Leaving control with other beneficiaries," Pinsley said, sounding thoughtful. "But that would only be temporary, and when it goes wrong, it can drain an estate. Killing her would be the next step."

He made it sound so logical, as if killing someone could ever be that, like there weren't emotions attached to all of it.

"I tried searching for any papers or journals or anything that would help," Kaia said. "There wasn't anything. Mrs. Hoyle says that the doctor who committed Tabitha took anything like that."

"It was good thinking to check," Pinsley said. "You did well, Kaia. We know more about Tabitha than we did."

That caught Kaia by surprise. She wasn't used to people praising her, however stiffly. Besides, it still felt to Kaia as if they didn't know enough. She'd been hoping to learn more about everything that was happening to her. Instead, she found herself digging up hints of inheritances and dead parents.

"What now?" she asked.

Pinsley considered for a moment. "It seems clear that the doctor is involved in this now. I think it's high time to see if he is in his office yet."

CHAPTER EIGHTEEN

Kaia felt a flicker of hope as she and Pinsley made their way back to Harley Street. There hadn't been many clues to be found in Tabitha's home, but at least they had the idea that she had been put in Bedlam for a reason. Maybe now, with the doctor, they might be able to find the truth of all this.

"So," she asked, "do you think that the doctor is in on what the family did, or would he just have been bribed to put Tabitha away?"

"It's best not to speculate," Pinsley said.

"But we found something," Kaia said. She found that, after that first glimmer of praise from him, she needed that recognition from him. "It makes sense, doesn't it?"

Pinsley's expression softened slightly. "It does, and I think what you found could prove important, but we need to be guided by reason. We cannot be so focused on what we think is happening that we risk missing what is actually happening."

Kaia could understand what he was saying, but even so, it felt to her as if they were getting close to the truth of all of this. They reached the doctor's home, and now when the inspector knocked on the door, a servant answered.

"I'm afraid the doctor is not seeing patients today," he said.

"We are not patients," Pinsley said, taking out his warrant card. To Kaia, his approach seemed slightly less terse than it had been with the housekeeper before. "We were hoping that it might be possible to speak to the doctor. We require his opinion on one of his patients."

"Come in," the servant said. "I will see if the doctor is able to speak with you."

He showed them into the house, along to a space that had apparently been repurposed from a sitting room to allow visitors to wait to be seen. There were a few hard chairs set out there, along with a series of marble busts of people Kaia couldn't begin to recognize, but who seemed to be famous physicians of the past according to the inscriptions: Galen and Vesalius, Hippocrates and Jenner. Kaia couldn't imagine having the money for that, or for a space just for

93

people to wait in, when the only space she'd ever had of her own had been the bedroom last night.

"Wait here a moment," the servant said, and then went over to a door on the far side of the room. He knocked and then went inside, returning a moment or two later. "Doctor de Vere will see you now."

Kaia followed Pinsley through into an office space that had a couple more of the same hard chairs set in front of a table covered in green leather. An assortment of brass devices were set out on it, presumably for use in examinations, while several weighty medical tomes sat on a shelf at one side. One was open on the desk, showing what appeared to be detailed drawings of the inside of the human body. Kaia didn't know whether to be disgusted or fascinated.

Then she looked up at the man standing behind the desk, and none of it was relevant anymore. She'd seen that avuncular face before, with its short white beard and curling white surround of hair, looking at her as she and Pinsley arrived at Bedlam.

The sensation from Bedlam hit her in almost the same moment: the sensation of something sinister there, something she couldn't put her finger on, but which was enough to make her shudder as she looked over at the doctor. There was something about him that frightened her, but it wasn't *just* fear, it was more than that. It was the sense of something wrong with the world, something that didn't fit.

"Good morning," he said. "Inspector Pinsley, wasn't it? My servant said that you wished to speak to me about one of my patients. Before we continue, I should point out that ethically, there are limits to what I can say, even to the police. The new General Medical Council are quite clear on that."

"I believe we have seen one another before, sir," Pinsley said. So *he'd* remembered the doctor too.

"Have we?" the doctor asked. Was it Kaia's imagination or did he barely glance away from her to Pinsley while he asked the question? His eyes returned to her, looking her over once more.

"On the steps of Bedlam," Pinsley reminded him. "Might I ask what you were doing there, sir?"

"Was it about Tabitha Greene?" Kaia asked. There, she'd caught the doctor off guard. She found that she liked the small hint of surprise in his expression.

"Do you often allow young ladies to ask your questions for you, Inspector?" the doctor said. Was that the reason for his surprise? Was he just startled that a girl could ask him a question?

"In this case, Kaia seems to have asked the right one," Pinsley said. "Please answer her, Doctor."

"Then yes," Doctor de Vere said. "I was there regarding Tabitha Greene. Following the… unfortunate circumstances of her death, I thought it best to visit and get the details for my records. A very sad end."

To Kaia, he didn't sound remotely sincere, and she found herself wondering if Pinsley saw it.

"What can you tell us of Miss Green?" Pinsley asked. "How did she come to be in the asylum?"

Now, the doctor was shaking his head, moving away from the desk. "That is information I do not feel that I should share. Her family-"

"Won't her family want to know the truth about what happened to her?" Kaia asked.

"And since Miss Greene is deceased," Pinsley added. "Ethical considerations of protecting your patients no longer apply. You are the doctor who brought her to Bedlam. Why?"

"Because it was the only place left for her," Doctor de Vere said, and again, Kaia noticed that his gaze stayed on her, rather than moving across to the inspector. "She exhibited delusions."

"Shadows moving on their own," Kaia said without thinking.

"And how do you know *that*, young lady?" the doctor asked. His gaze was piercing now, as if he might have dissected her there if he could.

"We have already made some enquiries," Pinsley supplied. Kaia guessed that the point was to provide an answer without giving too much away. But then, it seemed to her that the doctor was doing the same thing, like this was some kind of game.

"And did those enquiries tell you about the ways Miss Greene's delusions came to take over her life?" Doctor de Vere asked. "That she saw these shadows in every corner, and came to believe that the people who wanted to help her were being influenced by them?"

"Even so," Pinsley said. "It is a long way from that to putting her in Bedlam. Who asked you to do that, Doctor?"

Kaia was surprised by the directness of that question. Was the idea to see how the doctor reacted.

"Her own actions demanded it," Doctor de Vere said. "She attacked a man, screaming something about him being filled with shadows. He was not badly hurt, but he easily could have been. At that point, putting her where she could do no further harm was the only option."

Filled with shadows. Something about the words made a kind of sense to Kaia. She found herself staring at the doctor, that horrible sense of wrongness still seeming to fill her when he was too close.

"Tell me, young lady," he said. "What do you see when you look at me?"

"What?" Kaia said.

He smiled. "Only, you have been staring at me most intently. Is something wrong?"

He knew. He *knew* what effect he was having on her. Only... if Kaia said anything, she would sound mad now, like she was repeating Tabitha's own delusions. She might find herself dragged away to Bedlam just like Tabitha. Kaia knew that she couldn't say anything.

"No," she said. "Inspector Pinsley observes people so well that I thought I should try it."

Pinsley looked across to her, and Kaia could see the disbelief there. Still, he kept going with his questioning.

"Tell me, Doctor, have you received any remuneration from the family for placing Tabitha Greene in Bedlam?"

"Only what I am due for the consultations," Doctor de Vere replied. "I must say, Inspector, that I resent the insinuation that I may have acted in any way that was untoward."

He did a convincing impression of being genuinely hurt by the question, but Kaia could still feel the wrongness coming from him.

"I understand, sir," Pinsley said. "I had to ask the question, though. Did you visit Tabitha Greene in Bedlam?"

"From time to time," the doctor replied. "Will that be all, Inspector?"

Pinsley seemed to ignore the implication that he should leave. "And the nature of those visits?"

"Merely to ensure her continued wellbeing. I have been professional in this, and everything else, Inspector. Now, forgive me, but I have appointments. So I'll ask again, will that be all?"

To Kaia's surprise, Pinsley nodded.

"For now, sir."

He led the way from the room, and the house, leading Kaia out onto the street, and then away down Harley Street. As they got further away, the sense of wrongness Kaia had gotten from the doctor faded. She managed to wait until the end of the street before saying anything, but only with an effort.

"Why didn't you keep going?" she asked Pinsley.

96

"You think I should have kept questioning him?" Pinsley replied.

"He was obviously hiding something," Kaia said. She tried to work out how to explain what she felt around him. "There's something wrong about him, something… he pretends to be this civilized doctor, but there's something else about him. He's not who he seems."

"I agree," Pinsley said. He started to wave down a cab.

That caught Kaia completely by surprise.

"You agree? But we just left him! We could have-"

"Could have done what, Kaia?" Pinsley asked. "He was defensive enough as it was. If we'd kept going, he would simply have refused to answer more questions. Trust me, I have seen opium addicts before."

"You think he's an opium addict?" Kaia said.

"Ah, I thought you caught it," Pinsley said. "When you were staring at him, I thought that was why. He hides it well, but there is a slight shake to his hands, a little staining around his teeth from the pipes."

"I just thought that there was something *wrong* about him. Something he was hiding," Kaia said.

"Well, it is something that could be very embarrassing for a doctor," Pinsley said, "and something that might induce a man to lie. Addicts let their needs overrule logic and reason. It is entirely possible that Doctor de Vere is deeply involved in all this. Still, we need proof."

"And how do we get proof?" Kaia asked.

"The doctor told us one story about Miss Greene's incarceration in Bedlam. Your housekeeper, Mrs. Hoyle, told you another fragment of it. I suggest that we keep trying to get to the truth of that."

That sounded good to Kaia, because it meant that there was a chance of finding out more about the shadows Tabitha claimed to have seen and maybe… well, maybe why Kaia was seeing the same thing.

"How do we find out?" Kaia asked.

A cab stopped, and Pinsley hopped aboard. "I thought we would try talking to Miss Greene's family. Driver, to the railway station, if you please. We will need to catch a train urgently if we are to be there and back by nightfall."

CHAPTER NINETEEN

The being who had been the doctor sat with fingers drumming on his tabletop for long minutes, contemplating his position. The movement was an automatic one, a twitch from a body craving more opium. He ignored that for now.

His servant knocked and looked around the door.

"Your first appointment is here, Doctor de Vere," the man said. For the life of him, de Vere couldn't remember the man's name. He suspected that he hadn't been much interested in the names of servants even before, but now, all the elements of his life were jumbled things that felt as if they had happened to someone else. He could reach for them if he needed them, but it took an effort, and right now, the doctor had other things to concern himself with.

"Ask them to wait for a moment," de Vere said. He had no interest in a patient right now.

Things were spiraling out of control, and not just because of the cravings that still ran through de Vere. To have an inspector show up here, now, was unacceptable. It was understandable that there would be some police interest after the killing of Tabitha Greene, yet de Vere had assumed that the whole thing would be settled by now.

That had been the point of putting her there, after all. No one paid attention to what happened to those in Bedlam. Their own families wanted to forget them. Now, though, there was an inspector on his doorstep, asking questions, making insinuations… no, it would not do. If he dug too deeply, it might cause problems that de Vere was not currently positioned to deal with.

Doctor de Vere found that he was on his feet, halfway to the cabinet where he kept his medicines. He forced himself to go back to the desk. That wasn't the way to deal with this. He would think of something, but not that. That was the problem with having to join with the weak minded: their weaknesses persisted, even when the people themselves had long ceased to be what they were before.

The *real* danger, of course, didn't come from the policeman.

Did the girl know that she was a shadow-seer? Doctor de Vere had caught hints of it when he'd met her on the steps of Bedlam, but here, able to examine her for several minutes, he was confident of it. If one of her kind was interfering in his business, then suddenly everything that had seemed so settled might be in danger. *He* might be in danger.

True fear was a novelty for the doctor as he was now. Oh, he had memories of it, but it wasn't the same. He was stronger now than he had ever been, yet a shadow-seer could undo all that in a way that no one else might.

She hadn't said anything that suggested she knew, though. Obviously, she would need to be careful with an inspector beside her, but still, what if she didn't know what she was?

Tabitha hadn't known what she was. She hadn't known how much evil, hurtful, dangerous power had sat within her, and how much damage it could do to those whose shadows had extended to touch the human world.

Doctor de Vere snorted at that last thought. The *human* world? They swarmed over its surface like ants, brought painful light into places they shouldn't, but that didn't make it theirs. There had been darkness before the first light, after all.

"Doctor," his servant said. "The patient says that she has no time for delays."

"Yes, yes," Doctor de Vere said. "Show her in."

He barely even paid attention while he did his work these days. Who cared what ailed these people, or what their petty concerns were? He prescribed laudanum, of course. The more who took such opiates, the more possibilities there were for his kind. A weakened mind was easier to touch, and not all addicts had to be those begging for more in Limehouse opium dens.

"Thank you, Doctor. I'm sure this will help a lot."

They were always so grateful for it, as well. So grateful for a doctor who helped them, and gave them what they wanted, that they didn't think that de Vere might have his own reasons for it. Now though, he barely acknowledged his patient's gratitude. He had more important things on his mind.

What should he do about this new shadow-seer? If she knew what she was, and what he was, then direct action would be needed. The more he thought about it, though, the more certain de Vere was that she didn't know; she would have acted already if she did, and certainly wouldn't have allowed a police inspector near her affairs. Her kind didn't benefit from scrutiny any more than his.

That gave Doctor de Vere at least one good option, the same one that he'd taken when it came to Tabitha Greene. Someone who spoke about shadows and seeing things that others couldn't would always look mad to the poor, blind remainder of humanity. It would be worse for a girl like this Kaia, because de Vere doubted very much that she was from a good family, with money and status to make things more difficult for him. Getting her where he wanted would be easy.

In Bedlam the girl would be in a place where she could both do no harm and be reached easily, if necessary. Tabitha's death proved that much. Yes, Doctor de Vere decided, it was time to start making arrangements for this girl who didn't know what she was, just as he had for the last.

CHAPTER TWENTY

"You've never been on a train before," Pinsley guessed.

Kaia shook her head as they started to pass beyond the city, into the countryside beyond. "I've never been out of London, either. It's so *green* out here. Like one of the parks, but so much bigger."

Pinsley had to admit that the expression of wonderment on Kaia's face as they took the train out from London was almost enough to make the journey worthwhile by itself. He could see her watching the outskirts of the city flashing past through the smoke of the steam engine, and he smiled at her joy as she watched it all.

Pinsley had a harder time with the idea that there could be someone who had never seen the world beyond the sprawling streets of the Empire's capital. London had grown, even in the time when he'd travelled the world with the army, so that now people could spend their whole lives without ever setting foot outside its confines. The thought that Kaia had seen nothing of the world beyond a few streets made him feel sorry not just for her, but for all the others like her.

"How far is it?" Kaia asked. She didn't seem unnerved by the speed the train was moving at, but rather exhilarated by it.

The two of them sat together in a compartment. It reminded him of the last time he'd taken Olivia on a train, and although that thought brought pain with it, the reminder was also a surprisingly happy one.

"Perhaps forty miles," Pinsley replied.

"So far?" Kaia asked. "And we're really going to be back by tonight?"

Pinsley nodded. There were days when he was impressed by the ease of it all himself. "The journey should take perhaps an hour. There is a small station not far from the estate. If things go well, we will be back in plenty of time."

"And I'll be back in the vicarage?" Kaia asked. "Not the cells?"

"You have my word," Pinsley said. He didn't want to take Kaia back to the station now. In fact, given the choice, he would probably just let her go at this point. He couldn't shake the feeling, though, that he still needed her help with all this.

They waited while the train advanced its way through the countryside, coming to a halt at a spot where a newly built station stood, little more than a platform and a roof to keep the rain off, really. Pinsley and Kaia alighted, with him helping her down. There wasn't the parade of cabs that there might have been in the city, but Pinsley had sent a telegram ahead, and there was a coach waiting.

"Lord and Lady Greene's estate," he said, and the driver took them out through rolling hills. Kaia was still staring out at it all with obvious joy. Trees flashed past, and hedgerows, with men working the fields with shovels and hand plows, readying the February ground for the work of the year.

It was nothing compared to her expression when the manor house came into view. It stood at the end of a sweeping drive, among rolling expanses of lawn and with a lake at one side. The house itself was a huge, three winged affair, complete with the glass of an orangery on one side, and stables on another.

"It's bigger than... than Buckingham Palace," Kaia exclaimed, as the carriage continued towards it obviously stuck for any other point of comparison.

"Houses out in the country have more room to grow," Pinsley said, barely hiding a smile as they got close to the front doors of the place. He tapped on the side of the coach. "Here will do."

"The trade entrance is round the back," the coachman called back.

"Here will do," Pinsley repeated, biting back a flash of annoyance. It wasn't just the idea of being treated like he and Kaia weren't good enough for the front door. It was the lack of respect for the police that it represented. If he was just another tradesman to the aristocracy, then they could cooperate or not, as they deigned.

He and Kaia went to the front door, where they were met by a portly butler. Pinsley showed his warrant card.

"Ah, yes, sir," the butler said. "We've been expecting you. If you and your companion..."

"Kaia," Kaia said, clearly not wanting to be just that.

"...would care to come with me, I believe young master Dudley is in the billiard room at present."

"Dudley is..." Pinsley began.

"Cousin to the present Lord Greene, sir," the butler said, in a tone that suggested that anyone should know that.

He led the way across marquetry floors, past a series of portraits that seemed to be designed as much as a way of displaying the family tree as a way of decorating the place, in Pinsley's view.

"Who are all these people?" Kaia asked.

"The ancestors of the present Lord Greene, miss," the butler said. "Who were raised to their present rank after their efforts at Bosworth Field in 1485. Of course, the family traces its tree back further, through Agincourt and all the way back to Hastings, but it was the Wars of the Roses where they achieved their preferment."

Pinsley wondered what it would be like for an orphan who had never known her family, seeing so many of someone else's plastered across the walls. He put a reassuring hand on her shoulder, and she looked up in surprise.

They went through to a room where a man in his twenties was playing billiards. He wore no jacket, leaving him in shirt sleeves and a brightly colored waistcoat, red britches and yellow socks. A gold watch chain dangled from his waistcoat pocket, while his dark hair was somewhat longer than was fashionable, falling loose around his shoulders. A brandy glass sat on the side of the table. This was presumably Dudley Greene.

"Ah, Jones," he said. "Who have you brought?"

"Inspector Pinsley of the Metropolitan Police, sir," the butler explained. "And Miss Kaia."

"Ah, come to arrest us all, no doubt," Sir Dudley said with a laugh.

"Just to ask some questions," Pinsley said. He couldn't help a note of reproach creeping in at the lack of decorum. "Relating to the murder of Tabitha Greene."

"I'm sorry," Dudley said. "I shouldn't make jokes at a time like this. It's just my way. It's a terrible shock, what's happened to poor Tabby." He waved a hand magnanimously at the billiard table. "Please, ask whatever questions you like. Jones will fetch more brandy, or tea, or something. I don't suppose either of you plays? Inspector? Young lady?"

To Pinsley's surprise, Kaia hurried forward to take the cue Sir Dudley offered, and although she could never have played billiards before in her life, she lined up a shot.

"Could you tell us about the situation with Tabitha and her parents, please?" Pinsley asked while she was aiming.

It had to be the first time Kaia had played the game, but she got remarkably close, with the ball only bobbling out of the pocket at the last minute.

"Oh, bad luck," Dudley said. "It's hard to know where to start with all this, you know. There was the fire, of course, up at Loch Lomond. Do you know about that?"

"Where her parents died?" Kaia asked.

"Exactly," Dudley said, lining up his own shot. "A bad business all round. A terrible accident with the gas lamps, they say. And now there's all this business with poor Tabby. She was always a little fey, you know, even before Aunt Lily and Uncle James' deaths."

Pinsley leaned against the table, listening. Sometimes it was advisable to let people talk, and the young man in front of him seemed more than willing enough to share details. After a couple of days of searching in the dark for answers, Pinsley was grateful for it.

"They say she attacked someone," Dudley kept going. "Of course, you must have heard that. All hushed up, but still, she had to be put *somewhere*. I lobbied Quentin to make it Bath, or perhaps somewhere in Scotland, but he wouldn't hear of his sister being so far, so… well, you know where she ended up."

"I'm sorry," Kaia said. "Quentin is her brother?"

"Younger brother," Dudley said. "Your shot, I think."

"So if he was younger, would he have inherited much here?" Pinsley asked, trying his best not to make the question sound like an accusation.

"Oh, Quentin is the one who inherited the estate, the various shipping interests and so on," Dudley said. "Well, you know how these things go, male heir and all that, wanting to pass it all down through the line that would keep the family name if she married and so forth. Plus there's the seat in the House of Lords. Oh, very good," he added as Kaia sank a ball.

"So what *did* Tabitha inherit?" Pinsley asked. He needed to get a sense of the scale of what was involved.

"A couple of properties, of course," Dudley said. "The place in Bloomsbury, another over in Colchester, the ones that were more about keeping up with the Set than the businesses. Oh, and seventy thousand pounds."

Pinsley heard Kaia's intake of breath at that. Even he was impressed by it. Seventy thousand pounds was more than he could hope to earn in a lifetime. Inheriting that much would have made Tabitha

Greene not just comfortable for the rest of her life, but wealthy enough to do whatever she wanted.

"That's… a lot," Kaia said. "How did her brother feel about that?"

It was the question Pinsley couldn't ask, because it sounded too suspicious from an inspector, but from her, it just earned another laugh from Dudley.

"Oh, he was *furious*," he said, and switched to what Pinsley presumed was an impression of someone else. "'No woman should have that much money, Dudley! What will she do? Spend it on dresses?' He was quite put out. I think he saw himself administering a trust for her. He was all prepared for it until they read the will, you know. Said he'd give her a thousand a year. Could you imagine trying to live off a thousand a year?"

Since Pinsley earned roughly a fifth of that per year, before factoring in his army pension, he decided that it was better not to comment. Instead, he asked the obvious question.

"And where is Lord Greene now, sir?"

"Oh, he's gone up to London for a few days," Dudley said. "Taking his seat in the Lords, attending to a spot of business, that sort of thing." He raised his empty brandy glass. "I'm looking after the place."

"How *many* days?" Pinsley asked. Suddenly, it seemed like the most important thing in the world.

"Let me think. I think it was three days ago he left."

Pinsley saw Kaia look up at that. She'd obviously realized the importance of that too. Pinsley was impressed.

"And did he say where he was staying in London?" Pinsley asked.

"I'm afraid not," Dudley said. "There have been a few telegrams back and forth about Tabitha's death, but I really couldn't say anything more than that he's in London."

"I'm sure I'll find him, sir," Pinsley said.

He would make it his business to. From everything he'd just been told, Quentin Greene stood to gain an astonishing sum of money from his sister's death, *and* he'd been in the city at the time of his sister's death. Combine that with the role he'd played in putting Tabitha in Bedlam in the first place, and it was hard to escape the conclusion that he'd played some role in his sister's murder, using her cellmate as a convenient scapegoat.

How long would it be before they hanged Elsie for the killing? Pinsley didn't know, but he was all too aware that he was running out of time. He needed to track Quentin Greene down, and that meant heading back to London.

CHAPTER TWENTY ONE

Doctor de Vere stood outside Great Scotland Yard for a moment, brushing down his overcoat and making sure that his hair was neat beneath his hat. Given how observant the inspector seemed to be, it was important that he conveyed the right message in every line of his being.

Humanity cared so much about the way things appeared. They didn't look closer, or most of them didn't. Today, he would deal with at least two of those who did.

He walked into the police station, making sure that his expression was one of appropriate concern. He didn't even have to fake anger at what had happened, that was real enough. He shouldn't have to be here, doing this, rather than safe back in his office.

"Can I help you, sir?" a sergeant at the desk asked him as he approached, stepping past a couple of constables and whatever small criminals they were busying themselves with.

"I wish to speak to whoever is in charge here," the doctor said. "I have a complaint to make."

"If you tell me what's happened, I'll see to it that it's passed to an appropriate constable or inspector," the sergeant said.

"This is in *regard* to an inspector," de Vere said. "I have a complaint to make regarding Inspector Pinsley."

He saw the sergeant's expression shift, and knew that he'd said the right thing. The doctor's one worry with all of this was that Pinsley's fellow police officers would be too protective of him, and that he would then need to take other measures. One glance at the sergeant said that wasn't going to be a problem.

"You'll want to speak to Superintendent Hutton, sir," the sergeant said. "Woakes, show him up to the superintendent's office.

Doctor de Vere followed a young constable up a staircase, to the spot where a door stood solidly closed. A name plate on it said simply "superintendent," because apparently the rank was the only thing that mattered.

"Come," someone on the other side of the door said. The constable pushed the door open, stepping back to let de Vere pass into a wood

107

paneled office. The walls were decorated with awards, a picture of the queen, and another portrait that appeared to be Robert Peel. As soon as he clapped eyes on the uniformed man sitting bolt upright behind a mahogany desk, de Vere knew that he'd found the man he needed.

"Superintendent Hutton?" he said, stepping forward to meet him and extending a hand. "My name is Doctor de Vere, of Harley Street."

"Hello, sir," Superintendent Hutton said. "What can I do for you today? Typically our sergeants and constables handle enquiries coming in off the street."

"Sadly, I have an issue to raise regarding one of your inspectors. Inspector Pinsley."

Again, the reaction was gratifying. The superintendent was obviously trying to hold in his excitement at the words, but didn't want to be too obvious about it. That was something de Vere could work with.

"Please, take a seat," the superintendent said, gesturing to a chair on the other side of the desk.

The doctor sat, faintly amused by the decorum of it all. People were so indirect about everything, hedging around issues rather than confronting them head on. It created so many useful opportunities.

"I'm sorry to come to you with this," Doctor de Vere said. "But the way your man acted in my practice this morning was simply unacceptable."

"How so?" the superintendent asked.

"He practically forced his way into my offices, then started questioning me about the death of one of my patients, trying to get at information that I am required to keep in confidence as her physician."

"This would be Tabitha Greene?" Superintendent Hutton asked.

"He seemed… one hesitates to use the word 'obsessed' when one has seen the truly disturbed, but it seemed to me that he was more interested in wild conjecture involving Miss Greene's family than in the truth that she was killed by another poor unfortunate in Bedlam. If such things were to get back to Miss Greene's family, then I am sure they would find the whole thing most distressing."

"Investigations can be distressing," the superintendent said. "And while I do not always approve of Pinsley's methods-"

"Her brother is Lord Greene," Doctor de Vere said. "Who has recently taken up his seat in the House of Lords."

He had to suppress a smile as the superintendent stopped short. Of course someone in his position would be a political man, unwilling to rock the boat. The doctor decided to keep going.

"If there were any *real* question about poor Miss Greene's death, then of *course* we would all do everything we could to help," de Vere said. "But the only thing likely to result in this situation is a scandal that his lordship can hardly afford, with the political situation being so delicate."

"I quite understand," Superintendent Hutton said. "And really, this matter should have been resolved far more quickly than this."

"There is another aspect to it," Doctor de Vere said. "There was a young woman with the inspector, one who was being... well, she was behaving most oddly."

"There was a girl," the superintendent said. "A thief, who was due to go before the magistrate, until Pinsley decided that she was vital to his case."

"He decided it?" Doctor de Vere asked. "Or she convinced him?"

"I..." The superintendent paused, clearly unsure. Doctor de Vere decided not to give him more time in which to achieve clarity.

"It is my belief that this girl is quite deranged," he said. "She is a fantasist, spouting the most unbelievable things. In Pinsley, she found the one thing that all such people require: someone who will listen to and believe them."

"Yes, yes," Superintendent Hutton said. "I see it now. Why else would Pinsley simply take her out of police custody like that?"

"The girl gets to play out her fantasies of being someone special in a world that works according to her own absurd rules," Doctor de Vere said. "Your inspector gets a 'witness' or an 'expert' who knows things that conveniently point his investigation in the direction he wishes to examine. Tell me, Superintendent, does the inspector have any reason to have a grudge against Miss Greene's family?"

The superintendent frowned at that, and de Vere wondered for a moment if he'd gone too far.

"Not that I know of," he said. "Still, perhaps there might be something. Some slight from his army days perhaps, some family member given a promotion when he was not. You know what army men can be like when they are crossed."

Doctor de Vere smiled, because it seemed that he'd pitched it just right after all. "I have always steered clear of such men. So different from the police, of course."

"We take great pains to be different," Superintendent Hutton said. "And yes, I see this now. Pinsley took the investigation, and the moment he heard the victim's name, he saw a chance to bring scandal to the lives of her family. It's the only reason why he ignored such clear evidence that her roommate murdered her."

Doctor de Vere was surprised at how little of the work he'd had to do in this. Clearly, there was a depth of dislike in this man that he hadn't reckoned on.

"I will see Pinsley dismissed for this," Superintendent Hutton said. "His methods have always been worrying, but this is too far."

"And the girl?" de Vere asked. She was the one who mattered in all this, after all.

"Oh, she can face charges. She'll probably be transported or imprisoned."

In places where Doctor de Vere wouldn't be able to get to her. No, that wouldn't do.

"That seems a little harsh," he said. "After all, any crimes she has committed are likely to have come as a consequence of her insanity."

"Are you suggesting that we should simply leave her be?" Superintendent Hutton said, and de Vere was grateful for the sharp note in his voice there. A man who was *actually* prepared to let Kaia go would be no use to him at all.

"Of course not," Doctor de Vere said. "I am suggesting that we should put this girl into a place where her delusions can be treated. I will happily sign her into Bedlam, where she can get the help she so obviously needs."

"That," Superintendent Hutton began, "is very good of you, Doctor. Woakes!" The constable came running in. He'd clearly been waiting for Doctor de Vere. "Find Pinsley and the girl he took from here. Bring them here. Arrest them, if necessary."

CHAPTER TWENTY TWO

"So your plan is to find Tabitha's brother and question him?" Kaia asked as they stepped from the train. The station around her was a palatial thing, as if those building it had tried to make it as much like some grand ruin of ancient Rome as possible. A great glass and steel roof stood overhead, while the smoke from the trains filled the air, making it hard to pick out which way they were supposed to go.

"That's part of the plan, certainly," Pinsley said. "First, though, I want to go back to Bedlam."

Kaia swallowed as she heard those words. People poured out onto the platform around them, but she stood frozen to the spot. She didn't want to go back to that place, and the oppression she'd felt there. She could still remember the pall she'd felt over the place, the sense of utter wrongness there.

It was the same wrongness that she'd felt when it came to Doctor de Vere.

"I know the thought makes you uncomfortable, and if I could avoid it, I would," Pinsley said. "That place holds no more joy for me. Yet, if I am to accuse Lord Greene of killing his sister for her inheritance, I will need the kind of proof that can only be found there. Its documents may hold more secrets, or someone may be induced to speak."

"It wasn't about an inheritance!"

Those words came out before Kaia could stop them, seeming to hang in the air like the smoke from the engines pulling into the station. The inheritance might have been a huge amount, but she'd felt the darkness that hung around the doctor.

"Kaia," Pinsley said, taking a step or two into the crowd as if that would draw Kaia on, "he has a strong motive, he was in London, and he had a role in putting his sister in Bedlam. You yourself provided the idea that Miss Greene was placed in Bedlam specifically so that she could be murdered."

"By the doctor," Kaia said. She knew that she shouldn't be saying all of this here, in the middle of the station like this, but if she didn't, it felt as if she might burst. "When we met him, I felt something dark about him, something dangerous. I felt the same thing when we passed him on the steps of Bedlam."

"The man is clearly an addict," Pinsley said, "but that doesn't necessarily mean-"

"It's not that," Kaia told him. How could she hope to explain this to someone so wedded to reason? The inspector was starting to lead the way through the crowd, and Kaia had to follow, heading for the exit. "There's something *wrong* about him, something that doesn't even feel human. I think Tabitha saw that, and he killed her for it."

"There is no evidence of that, Kaia," Pinsley said, gently, as he might have to a child, while they reached the outer limits of the station. In its way, that was worse than if he'd been sharp with her.

"He was the one who put her there," Kaia said, trying to find some evidence that he might understand. "And back at the office, he was reveling in it. Remember when he asked me what I saw when I looked at him? He *knew* that I could see the strangeness in him, see that he-"

"Tabitha Greene was killed by a real, human murderer," Pinsley said, and his voice was firmer now. He started to call over a cab for the two of them. "Doctor de Vere is far from innocent in all this; I have no doubt that money changed hands to get him to commit Miss Greene to an asylum. Still, he has no motive."

"I can feel-" Kaia began.

"Feeling a thing is not the same thing as having proof of it," Pinsley said. "We live in an age of great advancements, and those have been brought to us by reason, Kaia. By evidence. The evidence here points to a man who thought that he could get away with killing his sister because her mind was unbalanced."

"But..." Kaia tried to think of something that might change his mind. Perhaps if she told him the truth of what had happened at the church? No, she couldn't. There was no way that he would believe it, and if she told him, she would only look stranger to him. "This is the wrong move."

"It is the *only* move," Pinsley replied. "We need to follow the evidence, which means that we need to go to Bedlam."

*

Kaia stared up at the central block of the asylum, trying to hold back her sense of disquiet. The strength of the wrongness she felt pushed at her, like it was trying to hold her out of there. Even so, she started to walk towards it with the inspector.

"You can stay out here if you wish," Pinsley said, gesturing to the rest of St George's Field. "I know that it was too much before."

Kaia knew that it was intended as a kindness, yet she couldn't go along with it. She couldn't be left out of all of this, and she didn't want the inspector to think that she was too weak to play her part in this. She shook her head.

"No, I'll come in," she said, taking another look up at the broad stone of the arch in which the door sat. She set her foot on the first of the steps before it, and forced herself forward. The moment they stepped inside, it felt as if she were being swallowed by the darkness of the place. She had to focus on the advancing form of the inspector just to make it inside.

They headed inside together, and instead of the warden being there, Kaia was surprised to see the keeper she'd seen the darkness in before, the one Pinsley had stayed behind to speak with. He had his arm in a sling, and Kaia could see the fear in his eyes when he saw them approaching.

Had the inspector done that? Kaia found herself a little shocked by that, but also quietly pleased, if it would do anything to stop this man from hurting more women.

"You can't be here," the keeper said, backing away from the desk in the middle of the lobby in obvious terror. "The warden-"

"The warden does not say if I may come and go," Inspector Pinsley said. "And I am more concerned with who *else* has come and gone here."

Kaia saw the keeper's face pale as those words struck home.

"N-nobody! Look at the log book if you don't believe me!"

He gestured to the book that sat on the table, but even Kaia could tell that he wasn't telling the whole truth. There was something else going on here. She could feel that, as clearly as she could feel the oppressive traces of something else there, something that lingered, making her feel unclean just standing there.

"I *have* looked at the log book," Pinsley pointed out, but he went to the table and flicked over the pages anyway. "And there really is no mention of anyone visiting Tabitha. Because you're all so keen on having people sign in, it's tempting to think that means that no one *did* get in."

"I don't know what you're getting at," the keeper said. "She was killed by her cell mate."

"He's lying," Kaia said. She could see that as clearly as she could see the fear on his face.

"You're letting girls speak for you now?" the keeper asked, and then fell silent as Pinsley took a step forward.

"Kaia is correct, though, isn't she?" Pinsley demanded. "You're lying to me. You know exactly what's going on here."

The keeper started shaking his head.

"Don't be so modest," the inspector said. "The warden said that you were the one to help with all the paperwork. No one *else* would be able to make someone disappear from the records, but you could, couldn't you?"

"I-" the keeper began.

Kaia went to the logbook, looking through it, going back through the pages. She'd found herself hoping that Doctor de Vere's name wouldn't appear, that he'd be able to get in without being noticed. No, though, his name *was* there for yesterday, for the visit he'd made where she had first felt the sheer wrongness of him.

"You can't mess with that!" the keeper said.

"Why not?" Pinsley countered. "You did. Someone came, didn't they? Someone with enough wealth and influence that he didn't have to sign. Someone who probably said that it would create a scandal if he did."

"I'm saying nothing," the keeper said.

"Really?" Pinsley asked.

"Break my other arm if you want to," the keeper said. "I'm not telling you who came here."

"You just confirmed that someone did, though," Pinsley said. "And in confirming it, you're caught up in it."

The keeper looked alarmed at that. "You arrest me, and I'll be out in a day. You touch me, and it will be your job."

Pinsley turned to Kaia, and she could see the look of triumph in his eyes. "Let's go. I think we have everything we need here."

"But I didn't tell you anything!" the keeper said.

"Oh, yes you did," Pinsley said, as he led the way outside.

Kaia hurried to keep up. She was grateful to be out of the oppressive atmosphere of Bedlam, but she was still confused as the two of them stepped out onto St George's Field.

"I don't understand," she said. "I thought you came here because you wanted to find evidence."

"Silence is a kind of confirmation, in this case," Pinsley said. "You saw how frightened he was of me, yet there was someone he was more frightened of."

Kaia nodded at that. She'd seen that part. "What does that mean, though?"

"Who could frighten him more than an inspector?" Pinsley asked her. "Who could get him out of trouble with the law? A member of the House of Lords, perhaps?"

To Kaia, it didn't seem much like definitive proof. Yet, to Pinsley, it seemed like confirmation of what he'd already been thinking. Kaia couldn't imagine Tabitha Greene's brother being responsible for the darkness she felt around Bedlam, though, just as she couldn't imagine the doctor *not* being a part of it.

"This still doesn't feel right," she said. "It doesn't feel like the truth of all of this."

"The truth is not a feeling," Pinsley said. "This is what we have the evidence for."

"So now you go and arrest Tabitha's brother?" Kaia asked.

Pinsley shook his head. "We do not have *that* much evidence, but we do at least have a reason now to approach a man who would be too important to bother otherwise. We can question him, put this to him, and if his answers are not adequate, *then* we can arrest him."

"So we go to find him?" Kaia asked.

"*That* is where we run into a problem," Pinsley said. "We know that he is in London, but we don't know precisely where. We can't exactly sit outside the Houses of Parliament, waiting for some chance glimpse of him, but it may be the only method we have."

Kaia was about to suggest that they get started when she realized something else. "I may know where he is."

Pinsley looked at her in surprise. "What? How?"

"Mrs. Hoyle mentioned that she looks after more than one property for the family," Kaia said. "She mentioned a house on Grosvenor Street that she keeps ready for visits. I bet *that's* where her brother stays when he's in London."

"It's certainly a possibility," Pinsley said, sounding pleased and surprised all at the same time. "Well done. *Very* well done, Kaia."

He hailed a cab, and leapt in, waiting for Kaia.

"Come on," he said. "We have a lord to question."

CHAPTER TWENTY THREE

"Get out of the way," Pinsley shouted as another carriage moved in front of them. Wealthy houses flashed by on either side, while plain trees lined the sides of the road, above the hustle and noise of the streets.

He could feel the urgency now as he and Kaia closed in on Grosvenor Street. They were so close to the answers now, and the prospect of finding the truth… well, it felt like going into battle had: both terrifying and strangely exciting all at once.

They came to a halt outside a row of tall, painted houses, each one looking modest enough from the outside, but probably larger on the inside than any two other homes in London put together. Pedestrians passed by on either side, and Pinsley looked around until he found a newspaper seller, a boy of probably no more than twelve. He flashed his warrant card, as discretely as he could, and then held out sixpence.

"Which of these is Lord Greene's house?" he asked. "Nod, don't point."

The boy snatched the sixpence out of Pinsley's hand as quick as a snake, then nodded to one of the houses. "That one, number twelve."

"Thank you," Pinsley said. He looked over to Kaia. "I want to do this quickly, catch him off guard. If we go in too diffidently, he will simply try to ignore us."

What he was about to do was a risk, but it was a justified one. With a man like this, they would need a confession, and the best way to get one was to go in, making it clear just how much they already knew.

"Are you ready?" Pinsley asked Kaia.

Kaia nodded, and together, they marched over to the door of Lord Greene's house, up the steps leading to it. Pinsley was a little surprised by how much he'd come to think of her as being almost like a partner in this, even though that was patently absurd. She was a civilian, and a young woman at that. Even so, he could not have gotten this far without her.

Taking a breath, Pinsley hammered on the door. When a servant opened it, he pushed his way inside, showing his warrant card in only the briefest flash.

"'ere, what do you think you're doing?"

"Where is Lord Greene?" Pinsley demanded.

The servant pointed to a drawing room. "But you can't-"

Pinsley was already marching towards it, with Kaia just a stride or so behind him. He threw the doors open, and got his first glimpse of Lord Quentin Greene. He was slightly overweight, with round features and a burgeoning stomach only barely contained by his waistcoat. His dark eyes were sunken into his face, and his dark hair was slightly unkempt. He was sitting on a couch, picking at a plate of food when Pinsley strode in, and he stood with his fork in his hand as Pinsley entered, holding it as if it might fend him off.

"Lord Quentin Greene?" Pinsley said. He had to admit that he was taking a certain amount of satisfaction in seeing Tabitha Greene's killer caught off guard like this.

"Obviously," the other man said. "And who are *you* meant to be? What do you think you're doing, storming into my home like this?"

"I am Inspector Pinsley of the Yard, sir," Pinsley said. "And I think that I am here to arrest you for the murder of your sister."

"For..." Pinsley saw Lord Greene's face redden. "How *dare* you, sir?"

"I dare because it's true," Pinsley said. "Today, I have been to your estate, and I have been to Bedlam. I have also spoken to the doctor you used to commit your sister there."

"I..." Lord Greene sat back down on the couch, looking as though Pinsley had struck him. "What do you know, or *think* you know?"

"We know that Tabitha was going to inherit a lot of money," Kaia said. "We know that you had her put in an asylum."

Lord Greene started shaking his head. "You know nothing. Who is this girl, asking questions of me, Inspector?"

"She is here aiding me," Pinsley said. He kept going. The trick was to not give the other man time to think. "We know that your sister was killed by someone who could get into Bedlam without leaving traces. We know that you had her put there. Admit it, you did it deliberately, knowing that it was a place where you could strike at her and blame it on another of the poor unfortunates there."

"I will admit no such thing," Lord Greene snapped back. "Because I *did* no such thing."

"We have the doctor," Pinsley retorted. "We can get the keepers to place you there. We know that you were in London at the time of her death and haven't been back to your estates since…"

"Because being there is too great a reminder!" Lord Greene roared. He went quiet, seeming to deflate a little. Pinsley had seen men about to confess before, knew the moment when their deflections fled.

"Tell me," Pinsley said.

"I did visit my sister," Lord Greene said. "And you're right, I arranged for it not to be in their idiotic log book, but I did so to avoid the possibility of scandal, not to cover up a murder. I pay the keepers there good money to ensure that, should some writer for the Telegraph or the Morning Post come sniffing around, they do not find anything to link a madwoman to me."

"That's not all of it," Pinsley insisted. "It can't be. Why go to see her *then*? What were you doing there, if it wasn't to kill her? Are you going to try to persuade me that you were merely there to visit your sister?"

"We know that you hated the fact that she'd inherited," Kaia put in.

"And that's why I went to get her to sign her share over to me!" Lord Greene shouted. "My parents had no *right* to leave her such a vast sum without control or conditions. If it weren't enough that she was a woman, my sister was always troubled. What if she gave the money away on a fancy? What kind of *damage* might she do with so much?"

"And you wanted the money," Pinsley said. He still wasn't ready to give up.

"I wanted to be able to afford to grow our family's interests," Lord Greene replied. "I wanted to be able to *protect* our family."

"I still have no reason to think that you did not kill her," Pinsley said. "That was the easiest way for you to regain control of the money, after all."

"You think that it would be *easy* for me to kill my own sister?" Lord Greene retorted. "The only blood I had left in the world, unless you count my idiot cousin."

"You put her in Bedlam," Kaia said, from beside Pinsley.

"I had to put her somewhere," Lord Greene said. "Do you know that she attacked someone?"

"We heard," Pinsley replied.

"When she did, I knew I had to do something with her," Lord Greene went on, "and I saw a chance to achieve two things at once. I put her there because I wanted to put pressure on her; I'll admit that much. I gave her a brief time there, to see what it could be like, and then I went to her with a document that my solicitor had drawn up, one that would give me a complete power of attorney over her affairs, in exchange for taking care of her in a more refined environment."

"A more refined environment?" Pinsley asked. He tried to hide his disgust at the thought of a man who could put his sister in a place like that simply to put pressure on her.

"One of our country houses, or perhaps the town house in Bath," Lord Greene said. "She would be given quiet, servants, an allowance… everything that she should have been given under the control of a trust. I am not a cruel man."

"Not cruel?" Kaia said from the side. Pinsley could hear her disbelief, and her anger. Too late, he realized what that might mean. She stepped forward, and Pinsley wasn't fast enough to keep her from slapping the nobleman. The sound of it rang around the room.

Pinsley stared at Kaia in shock. Did she not understand who she had just struck? The potential repercussions of the action made his blood run cold.

"How dare you?" Lord Greene demanded, and lifted his hand as if he might strike her in return, but Pinsley recovered in time to step there between them then.

"Please," he said, thinking quickly. "*Show* me how easily you commit violence against young women."

"I've already explained," Lord Greene said. "I was there to get my sister's signature."

"So you've said," Pinsley said. He didn't bother to keep the disbelief out of his voice. "But I have yet to see any evidence of that."

"That is easy enough," Lord Greene said. "You see, Inspector, my sister *did* sign the document."

He went over to a bureau, unlocking it with a small key that he took from his pocket. As he reached into it, Pinsley tensed, because there was always the possibility that he might come out with a weapon. His hand closed over his truncheon, just in case.

Lord Greene came out holding a document, though, and held it out to Pinsley. The inspector took it, holding it up to examine the neat copperplate set out by a solicitor. Skimming over it, Pinsley could see that it was everything Lord Greene had claimed it to be, right down to the signature at the bottom.

"This could be a forgery," Pinsley said, but even he knew that he was clutching at straws.

"Compare it to any letter my sister has written," Lord Greene said. He took a sheaf of other papers from the bureau, all but flinging them at Pinsley. Pinsley only had to glance at them to know that they were in the same hand as the signature.

"So, why was your sister still there?" he asked. "Why was she stuck in Bedlam?"

"Because such things take *time,*" Lord Greene snapped back. "Securing her release and having it all be legal would have taken a judge and a friendly doctor. It would have taken a day or two. My great shame in all this is that I thought she would be safe there for that long. If I had taken Tabby out of there immediately and damned the consequences, my sister might still be alive! Believe it or not, Inspector, I loved my sister."

The worst part of it was that Pinsley did believe him, and that meant that he'd been so very, very wrong about all of this. That thought felt like a house of cards collapsing in his head, so that Pinsley didn't know what to think. He'd thought his logic was impeccable, and now... he'd gone wrong somewhere, but he couldn't think where.

"I think I have indulged this long enough," Lord Greene said. "Get out of my house, unless you plan to arrest me for something."

Pinsley thought about trying it; it was still wrong, what his lordship had done, but proving a crime now, with his sister dead so that she couldn't say that she'd signed under duress, would be difficult.

"Come along, Kaia," he said.

"But-" She obviously didn't want to give this up either.

"We have to go," Pinsley said, leading her towards the door.

"This is not over, Inspector. I have been struck in my own home, and accused. I will not tolerate it."

With every step, he found himself going over the reasoning that had led him to this. He'd gone wrong somewhere, but he couldn't see where.

Worse than that, he didn't know what he was meant to do next. He'd failed.

CHAPTER TWENTY FOUR

Kaia hurried after Pinsley, who barely seemed to be looking her way as he walked along, back in the direction of Camden Town. He seemed to be muttering to himself, and had taken out his pocket watch, as if there might be some clue to all of this in the ticking of the thing.

"What are you doing?" Kaia asked.

"I don't know," Pinsley replied. "That's the point."

He kept walking, kept ignoring her as he looked at his watch.

"Why are you staring at the watch?" Kaia asked him.

"It helps me to think. Things have gone wrong somewhere. *I've* gone wrong somewhere. But the chain of logic is impeccable. Who else *benefits* from this death?"

Kaia was pretty sure that he wasn't talking to her by the end of that. He was talking to himself, barely looking where he was going, so that the people who passed them had to jump out of the way to avoid Pinsley walking straight into them.

"Sorry, sorry," Kaia said, apologizing to them one after another as she tried to keep up with the inspector.

"There has to be another explanation," Pinsley muttered to himself.

Kaia saw her chance to help. "There *is*," she said. "Remember what I told you about the doctor?"

Pinsley didn't even answer her this time. He was still muttering to himself, quieter now, moving his hands in the air as if he could place the facts in front of him to examine them like a butterfly under a pin.

For the first few seconds, it was fascinating to watch, but after that, the main thing Kaia felt looking at it all was just how excluded she was by the obsession of Pinsley's approach. He'd kept her on the sidelines for so much of this, had only just started to let her play any real role in all of this, and now here he was, not even talking to her.

Kaia knew that she had to try. "What I felt about the doctor, it's real. I felt it when I found Reverend Faulkner being attacked in the church."

"Kaia, I need to concentrate," Pinsley said.

"I'm trying to help," Kaia said. "I need to tell you the truth of what happened in the church. You need to understand what this is really about. I didn't just *hear* something happening in the church: I felt it, like I felt what was wrong with the doctor. Then, in the church, it was like a pressure building up inside me and…"

Pinsley was still walking, still muttering away to himself. Kaia knew then that he hadn't heard a word she'd just said. Either that, or he didn't believe it. Kaia had been frustrated enough before when he had ignored her to go chasing after Tabitha's brother. Now though, she could feel that frustration boiling over. If she didn't get him to listen, the real killer was going to get away with all this, and Kaia couldn't allow that, even if Reverend Faulkner had told her not to tell Pinsley about all of this.

Making up her mind, she stepped into his path, putting a hand out to stop him.

"Stop!" she said. "Stop and *listen* to me!"

"Listen to what?" the inspector asked. He looked at her directly, and now there was a challenge in his expression. "To stories about how you've felt this or that, and so I should base my entire investigation on it?"

"You're not going to do that," Kaia said, raising her voice. A few people glanced over, then kept walking quickly, obviously embarrassed by the disturbance. "You're not going to treat the things that have happened as if they're nothing. I know what I felt when-"

"You *think* you know," Pinsley said. "But I have to base my investigation on more than just imaginings."

"They are *not* imaginings!" Kaia shouted at him. "In the church *I* was the one who blew out the windows, me, without touching any of them! What do you think of that, Inspector?"

"I think that I was wrong to get you so tangled up in all of this," Pinsley said. "I saw a birthmark, and I assumed that it must mean something. I brought you along, but doing that has brought me no closer to the killer. Instead, it has distracted me, led me astray somewhere, and now you are talking about nonsense that has no place in a rational world."

"You're talking like it would have been better to leave me in a cell," Kaia said, venting her anger at the way Pinsley dismissed everything she thought and felt.

"Perhaps it would have been," Pinsley snapped back. "At least then, I might be able to *think*."

Kaia stood there, not knowing how to react to that. She couldn't believe that he'd actually said something like that. Didn't he understand what would have happened to her if he hadn't intervened?

She wanted to shout something at him, wanted to make him understand just how wrong he was about all of this, but she couldn't work out how.

She was still trying to work it out when a pair of other policemen approached: big men, in their full uniforms.

"Inspector," one said. "Superintendent Hutton sent us. We have been looking for you all over London."

*

Pinsley stared at the officers, surprised that Hutton would bother sending men out specifically to find him.

"What is it?" he demanded. "Has there been a development in the case?"

"The superintendent has given orders that you are to return to Scotland Yard immediately, sir," one of the constables said.

"Very well," Pinsley replied. Whatever this was with the superintendent, he would deal with it. His mind still raced, trying to work out what it might be. Had there been another murder? In the most crowded city in the Empire, perhaps the world, there was always death there to find. "I will return this young lady to her lodgings, and then-"

"The superintendent sent out orders regarding the girl as well," the other constable said. "It has been determined that she is both dangerous and mad, so we are to take her to Bedlam at once."

"Bedlam?" Pinsley said, not quite able to believe it.

Kaia's reaction was much stronger. "No, you're not taking me there. This is the doctor. He's done this!"

Pinsley saw her start to back away.

"Come along quietly, Miss," one of the constables said. The two of them advanced on her. "You should be grateful. It's better than transportation, isn't it?"

"No, it's not," Kaia shouted back, looked over at Pinsley. "Help me!"

Pinsley winced. He wished that he could do something, but he knew what it would mean. Kaia was an arrested criminal. If Pinsley intervened now, he would be in dereliction of his duty. He was a police inspector, and if that meant *anything*, then he had to stand back now.

Except that he knew that Kaia was innocent, and she very definitely wasn't mad. He couldn't allow this to happen.

"That's quite enough!" he said. "Step away from her!"

Kaia was already trying to fight back as the constables grabbed for her. He saw her kick out at one with a booted foot, catching him in the knee, then strike out at the other with a fist.

"Leave her, I said," Pinsley ordered.

It wasn't enough to break her free. Instead, it meant that the two constables bore Kaia to the ground, screaming and thrashing about, trying to break free of their grip. Pinsley started forward, determined to intervene. Around them, people on the street stopped to stare at the disturbance, and seeing that hurt Pinsley as much as the rest of it. Kaia shouldn't be an object of entertainment for those who thought they were better than her.

That was exactly what she *would* be in Bedlam. They would come and stare at her, and she would be in a place where Pinsley already knew how some of the keepers acted. He knew how terrible a fate this would be for her, even compared to being taken before a magistrate and convicted for the theft that had brought her into all of this.

Pinsley couldn't stand by and let that happen, even if it meant laying hands on the constables in violence. He took another step towards the melee, determined to put a stop to all of this. The two constables were pinning Kaia down, holding her there in spite of her efforts to break free. One of them reached for his handcuffs, and Pinsley reached out to grab that arm and order them to let Kaia go. Whatever else was true, he still outranked these constables.

The scream that came from Kaia in that moment seemed larger than anything any human body could hope to contain. There was a kind of physical force to it, a power that seemed to billow out from Kaia in a wave of something Pinsley couldn't begin to explain.

That force struck him, sending Pinsley staggering from his feet. He tumbled as if a hurricane had caught hold of his overcoat, rolling as he fell and feeling the pain of bruises rising across his body.

The two constables trying to hold Kaia were thrown back even more violently. Pinsley saw them flung through the air as if they weighed nothing, despite the fact that they were large men. They tumbled out into the street, and one of them only barely avoided rolling under the wheels of a milkman's cart.

Pinsley could only lie there stunned for a moment, and not just because he'd hit his head as he landed. He couldn't believe what had just happened, couldn't believe that Kaia had somehow just managed to send two constables flying, along with him. It made no sense, and certainly didn't fit into a rational world.

Even as Pinsley lay there, trying to make some sense of it all, Kaia was already pulling herself to her feet. Pinsley wanted to call out to her and tell her not to go, but he was too stunned for that in that moment. In any case, he wasn't sure that she would listen to him. Why should she, when he was just another one of the police sent to drag her away?

He could only watch as she ran off, into the city. Starting to pull himself to his feet, Pinsley wondered if he should go after her. No, though, it was better to let her go. She was better off out of all of this.

Pinsley waited while the constables got to their feet as well. They looked around.

"Which way did she go?" one demanded, but didn't wait for an answer. He and the second constable set off into the crowds of people around them, taking out their police issue rattles to try to summon assistance as they went.

Pinsley didn't join in the chase. He couldn't bring himself to do it. If he could think of a way to help Kaia, he would be doing that right now, instead. There was nothing he could do, though. He could barely think, after whatever had just happened. All he could do was hope that Kaia would get away.

As for himself, he had his own problems. He had his orders. He needed to go back to the Yard, and report to Superintendent Hutton. Given what had just happened, he was *not* looking forward to it.

CHAPTER TWENTY FIVE

Kaia stumbled off blindly into the heart of London, not knowing what to think or feel, only knowing that she needed to get away. Behind her, she could still hear the rattles of the policemen trying to find her, and that spurred her to keep running.

Her eyes misted with tears. She felt so hurt, so betrayed. Pinsley had promised her that he would let her go for her help, but he hadn't even *tried* to help her. If anything, he'd been coming over to help arrest her when she'd...

What *had* she done? Kaia couldn't make sense of the way she'd managed to fling three grown men away from her. It had felt like something had been building up inside her, with all the frustration, and the fear, and more pushed down until it had exploded.

It was the way things had been back in the church. There, Kaia had felt the power rising up in her in response to the awful wrongness that she'd felt coming from the shadowy figure in front of her. Here, it had come out because she'd been pinned down, and trapped, but it still didn't make any sense.

Kaia kept pushing her way past people, taking turns at random. Running in her hooped skirts and corset was easier than she'd thought it might be. Even so, Kaia knew that she couldn't run forever. She had to find somewhere safe. She thought that she could see Westminster Abbey in the distance, and Kaia headed towards it. She didn't know why, except perhaps that it was some instinctive thought of the church as a safe place, brought on by her time at St Michael's.

She dove across the street, dodging between two carriages. A horse whinnied and reared, so that hooves flashed close to her face. Kaia barely avoided them, and kept running.

She couldn't go back to the vicarage now, of course. People would look for her there. It would be almost the *first* place that Pinsley looked. Kaia headed in the direction of the abbey, making sure that she didn't slow down, even for a moment.

The rattles of the constables were growing fainter, and glancing behind herself, Kaia could no longer catch glimpses of blue uniforms among the people there, even if she could still see the ripples of where she'd run in the people who turned and pointed, or shouted in her wake.

Kaia slowed to a walk now, but a determined one, so that it would be less obvious which way she'd gone. Above her, the sky was getting darker, and fog was rolling in off the river, making everything around Kaia harder to see. She was grateful for all of it, because it meant that no one would be able to hunt her down now.

Around her, the grand buildings of Westminster gave way to a tangled web of streets whose buildings seemed to lean in on one another, blocking out the little light that was left. Tenements rose up on either side, with strings of washing hung between them like bunting.

Kaia kept going, but she was well past the first rush of flight, and now she found too many thoughts and feelings intruding on her. Betrayal, at the way Pinsley hadn't stepped in to save her, confusion, at what had happened back there, but also a deeper sense that there was so much more to this than she could dream of. Last night at the church had been strange enough, but to do it again, out in the middle of the street where everyone could see her was something else entirely.

Kaia needed to get *off* the street now. She was tired, and she didn't think that it was just from the running. It felt like whatever she had done to the police constables had drained something in her, something that would need time to recover. She couldn't do that out in the open, though, because there was too much of a chance that the police might find her, and in any case, it was starting to rain.

Kaia sought cover, finding it in the space underneath one of the bridges by the river. Was it Westminster Bridge? She huddled there, trying to keep out of the cold, and somewhere, in all of it, she found herself falling asleep.

*

Pinsley was still worrying about Kaia as he stepped into the Yard. Would the constables have caught her by this point? He found himself hoping that they hadn't. Let her escape to somewhere beyond London. Maybe she would be able to find a life for herself out in the wider country. Certainly, it seemed better than what awaited her if she was caught.

Yet there was still the question of what had happened back there, and exactly how she'd managed to do it. That question bothered Pinsley, because no matter how he turned the situation in his mind as

127

he stepped into the station at Great Scotland Yard, he couldn't find the rational explanation behind it.

The sergeant at the desk nodded to him, gesturing to the stairs leading up towards the offices.

"The superintendent is waiting for you, sir," he said. "He said that you were to go straight up."

Pinsley tried to read the sergeant's expression, to guess at what the superintendent might want. There was concern there, but not of the kind that he might have expected if there had been another killing. Yet Hutton wouldn't have demanded his present for something minor.

Pinsley went upstairs, striding to the superintendent's office and knocking sharply on the door. Better to get whatever this was out of the way, so that he could focus again on finding Tabitha Greene's killer.

"Come!" Hutton called from beyond the door, and from the moment he opened it, Pinsley knew that it wasn't going to be as simple as he'd thought.

The superintendent wasn't bothering to hide an expression of triumph. He was sitting there, looking at Pinsley as if trying to drink in this moment for future reference.

"Inspector," he said, taking a sheet of paper out as if he had some damning evidence of a crime. "You've finally gone too far."

"Sir?" Pinsley said, stepping into the room.

"You've been harassing innocent members of the public, on the word of some mad girl," Hutton said.

"I do not believe Kaia to be mad," Pinsley replied.

The superintendent stood. "What you believe is not relevant here. I warned you when you took that girl from custody that the consequences of it would be on your head."

Pinsley stood there. He suspected, at this point, that it didn't matter what he said. Even that proved to be the wrong thing.

"Well?" Hutton demanded. "Have you nothing to say for yourself?"

"I have yet to hear any accusation that I have acted in a way that I should not, sir," Pinsley said. In a moment, he'd gone from being a police inspector back to being a soldier standing in front of some superior. He even found his feet wanting to come to attention. He stopped himself. Hutton didn't deserve that level of respect.

"That you have acted... you harassed people of quality, you made baseless accusations... we've had *complaints* about your conduct, Pinsley."

Pinsley swallowed at that thought. "With respect, sir, when we went to question Lord Greene-"

"You questioned a member of the House of Lords?" Hutton demanded, his voice rising. To Pinsley, it sounded a little like he might explode. "You dared... at a time like *this*?"

"No one is above the law, sir," Pinsley said. "And the evidence implicating him in his sister's death-"

"What evidence?" Hutton shouted. "The ravings of some mad girl? Your own imaginings, passed off as reason?"

"Since Tabitha Greene was clearly killed by someone from the outside," Pinsley began, trying to explain it all, "and there was no sign of any visitor in the asylum's log book-"

"Your so called evidence is an *absence* of evidence?" the superintendent said. He shook his head. "No, enough of this. It was bad enough when the only complaint against you was from a respected doctor, but harassing a lord as well? Even the Commissioner won't protect you from this. You're suspended from your post, Pinsley, effective immediately, while an enquiry takes place into your conduct?"

"An enquiry?" Pinsley said. In spite of himself, anger rose up in him. "I've done *nothing* except try to find the murderer of a woman who-"

"Who was killed by her cellmate!" Hutton bellowed back at him. "That much was obvious from the start of all this. But no, the magnificent Pinsley of the Yard had to see more in all of this, some grand plot that would prove his brilliance compared to us mere mortals."

"Compared to you, sir?" Pinsley said. If he was being suspended, he saw no reason to hold back. "I wouldn't have thought that it would take that much."

"I'll have your job for this, Pinsley," Hutton snapped at him. "You'll be lucky if you don't see the inside of a cell for it. As for the matter of Tabitha Greene, it is done. Constables are going even now to formally arrest her roommate. She'll go before the magistrate in the morning, and mad or not, she'll hang for this. Then it will be done."

That part horrified Pinsley. He couldn't let it happen.

"You're going to hang the wrong woman," Pinsley said.

"So you say," Hutton said, "and what *you* say has no relevance here, Pinsley. Leave your warrant card and your truncheon, then get out of my station. If I see you here again before the enquiry is concluded, I *will* have you arrested."

Pinsley thought of all the things he might say in response to that, and realized that any retort he might have would be wasted on the superintendent. Instead, he set his warrant card and truncheon down, turned and stalked out from the station, not stopping until he was back in the open air.

He walked away through the dark of London, trying to think. The weight of what had just happened sat around his neck like a millstone. Pinsley had just been suspended, pending an inquiry into his conduct. He had no doubt that Hutton would do everything he could to see him dismissed. With the way things were going politically, he would be lucky to come through that attempt. After the service he had put in, it was too much.

He knew that he should just return to his club, or to his home. He should wait out all of this. A part of him longed to do that, to simply step away from a force that was so blind to the truth. He'd done everything he could to make things better for years. He'd fought for his country, and he'd hunted down criminals. It had cost him his wife, his daughter, and now even the job itself. Hadn't he earned the right to just stop?

Pinsley knew that he couldn't, though, because if he did that, Tabitha's roommate Elsie was going to die.

She didn't deserve that. Pinsley didn't know who had committed the murder, but he was still certain that she hadn't played any part in it. There was far more going on here than some petty squabble in Bedlam.

As he walked, Pinsley found his attention returning to Kaia. She didn't deserve any of this, either. Every time he thought of her, it reminded him of his daughter, Olivia. If she were the one running through London, trying to stay ahead of the police, he would be terrified for her.

He couldn't stop thinking about the way she'd thrown off the constables. There had been a power there that was... Pinsley could think of no better word than "uncanny." It was a disturbing thought, one that went against everything that he believed about the world. A part of Pinsley wanted to ignore it, even now.

Yet a part of being a rational man was accepting the truth when one saw it. Pinsley had seen what Kaia could do, had felt it for himself. The implications of that were vast. If she truly did possess some power, then maybe she could do other things too. Maybe those feelings of hers *meant* something.

He'd decided before that she was no part of this, yet now, he couldn't help feeling that she was at the very heart of it all. At the very least, she was alone and in danger. He needed to find her, both to protect her from the possibility of being thrown into Bedlam and to find the truth behind all this.

First though, he needed to return home. Pinsley had a feeling that this was going to be dangerous, and that meant... well, there was something he needed to collect.

CHAPTER TWENTY SIX

Kaia slept, and as she slept, she dreamed of shadows moving, weaving like snakes amid the mists of London. It wasn't just London, though. Kaia saw the streets that looked completely different, and places that didn't have streets at all. She saw forests and deserts, saw the pyramids of Egypt and the ruins of what had to be Greece.

The locations barely mattered. What mattered were the shadows. They were everywhere that humans were not looking, extending from patches of darkness, reeling away whenever the light touched them. She saw some caught by lamps or candles, saw spots where great fires had been built out in the wilds, shadows dancing on their edges.

Kaia understood now why people had always feared the dark. There was a power in it that was dangerous, that was cruel, that…

She didn't know what it was, but still, she saw the shadows moving, and now, in her dream, those shadows converged, becoming a pool, a wave that headed towards her, and washed over her, and…

Kaia woke with a start, as a hand shook her shoulder. It was still dark, and in the darkness she thought for a moment that the shadows were still closing in on her. Then she felt the cold, saw the stones of the bridge, and remembered where she was.

That didn't make the presence of shadowy figures so close to her any better. Kaia started to stand up with a start, but a strong hand pushed her back down.

"No point getting all het up, lovely," a man said, in a too jovial voice. "Don't go getting up on our account."

"What?" Kaia said, as more hands grabbed at her. "Who are you? What are you doing?"

"What do you reckon, Ben?" the one who was talking asked.

"Nice enough piece," another said. He was a big man, and his accent wasn't London. He sounded… Irish, maybe? "Nice clothes. Nice face. Mrs. Whitter will give us a couple of guineas for something like this."

Kaia recoiled in fear. "You can't-"

"Think anyone's going to look for her?" the first one asked, ignoring Kaia.

"Not if she's sleeping under a bridge," the Irish one said. "Come on, girl."

He grabbed for her, and Kaia tried to wrench free. "You can't do this," she said. "The police-"

"Where we're taking you, the police won't care, girl," the one who'd grabbed her said.

The other one grabbed her other arm, taking out a scarf and starting to wrap it around her wrist.

Kaia found herself thinking about what had happened with the police constables before, and in the church. She *had* the power to get these men off her, if only she could find it. She reached down into herself, trying to get it to rise up and fling these men away.

Nothing happened. Underneath the terror, there was no power, only the exhaustion that had forced Kaia into sleep in the first place.

That left trying to fight normally, and when Kaia tried to scratch and kick her way free, the men holding her only laughed.

"Help! Somebody help me!" Kaia screamed out, and the sound carried through the fog of London, but not for long. One of the men stuffed another scarf into her mouth, muffling her cries.

She tried to fight, with every scrap of her strength, but without the power that had saved her before she *wasn't* strong. She was small and light enough that even one of these men could have carried her off. Two at once meant that in seconds, Kaia found herself bundled down to the ground, her hands bound behind her.

They dragged her up to her feet, and threw a coat around her shoulders to disguise the fact that she was tied. One of them grabbed each of her arms, and from the outside, in the fog, it must have looked like they were just helping a friend home through the dark.

They dragged Kaia away, and all she could do was cry out in muffled fear.

*

Pinsley moved through the London night with all the speed he could muster. It was a different city in the night, lit by lamplight, but it was still far from empty. The theatres were open instead of the shops, and public houses were resounding to the sounds of revelry instead factories belching smoke. There were fewer hawkers out on the street,

133

but there were still figures lurking in the darker corners to trap the unwary.

Pinsley moved among them, and even if he didn't have his warrant card now, they still knew him. He went to the spot where he'd lost Kaia, working on the basis that it was the best place to pick up her trail again.

"There's a girl I'm trying to find," he said, stopping at a spot where an old soldier was begging on a street corner, one leg covered in bandages.

"Plenty of girls round here," the man said.

"And I'm looking for a specific one," Pinsley said. "If you don't start being helpful, Willie Cribbins, I'll start explaining in a loud voice exactly how obvious your tied up leg is. Maybe I'll cut your bandages off, and you'll have a miraculous recovery."

"There's no need to be like that," the old soldier said. "Not my fault if I didn't get my leg blown off. *Could've* had, if only-"

"The girl," Pinsley said. "One who was running away from the constables earlier, near here."

"Oh, I *heard* about that," the man said. "Pushed over a couple of your constables, didn't she? Caught them flat footed and ran."

Pinsley smiled to himself at how efficiently any hint of the uncanny had been erased from the story by London's rumor mill.

"Which way?" Pinsley asked.

"Hard to say," the soldier said.

Pinsley reached down for his bandages.

"All right, all *right*. They reckon Westminster. That's all I have, I swear."

Pinsley nodded, and moved on. Information in a place like London was like its fogs, usually found in wisps, occasionally obscuring everything. He stopped again, a pace from an urchin sitting on the steps of the abbey. He tossed the boy a shilling's worth of pennies and ha'pennies.

"A girl," he said. "Who came through this way earlier, running from the peelers."

"Like you, you mean?" the young boy asked.

"You've sharp eyes," Pinsley said. "If your friends have eyes as sharp, I've another half a crown for you. This isn't police business, and there's no trouble for you and yours."

The urchin seemed to consider that, and then ran off into the fog. Pinsley swallowed back his worry, trying not to think about the possibility that the boy was already laughing about the shilling he'd gotten for nothing from a stupid policeman. If it came to that he wasn't sure what to do next.

Willie Cribbins had said "Westminster," but that took in plenty. Pinsley couldn't imagine that Kaia had found shelter in the Houses of Parliament or in Westminster Abbey, and most of it was too wealthy to tolerate even a well-dressed orphan looking for charity, but there were still plenty of nooks and crannies, niches and doorways where she might hide.

He had to find her. It wasn't just that Pinsley needed her for this case, he was worried about her. Kaia might have abilities that he had no way to explain, but she was still a girl without a family, out on the streets. If she'd fallen in with a gang of thieves, or worse... Pinsley wasn't sure that he would be able to forgive himself.

Almost inexorably, he found his eyes being drawn to a cluster of streets that stood out as a particularly blighted carbuncle against the grandeur of Westminster. Surely Kaia would know not to go near there? Then again, if she wanted to avoid the police, where would be better to do it than the space known as the Devil's Acre? Constables didn't patrol there, and only went there at all in numbers. Even Pinsley usually drew the line at its edges. Going in there would be like going into battle again. Already he could feel fear rising, but not for himself.

Pinsley looked in doorways and behind walls as he passed. It was so easy to walk past them without seeing; most people did. Here and there, faces looked back at him as London's homeless found their spots for the night.

Pinsley's heart dropped as he checked the space beneath Westminster Bridge. He could see signs of a scuffle here, and a recent one. The mud beneath it was disturbed, and there were scraps of cloth where a dress had caught against the stone. Pinsley lifted them, and they were far too close to those of Kaia's dress for his liking. To quell his rising panic, he had to remind himself that it *might* mean nothing; not every fight in London was related to Kaia.

Even so, if she'd been this way, and stumbled into a space that had been claimed by someone else, maybe this fight had seen her hurt, or worse. What if she'd gone into the filth of the Thames? What if her body was floating down it even now?

A small figure came running up, and Pinsley knew that he was letting too much emotion show on his face when the urchin stopped short, looking at him nervously.

135

"You took forever to find again, you did," the boy said. "Then I figured 'he's an inspector, so maybe he's looking here already.'" He held out a hand expectantly.

Pinsley took out a half crown. "When you tell me what I need to know."

The urchin hesitated, looking round as if trying to decide whether it might be better to run off into the fog again. Pinsley knew then that he wasn't going to like what he heard next.

"What is it?" he asked.

"Little Tom said he saw a couple of hard nuts grab a girl here," the boy said. "He said they worked… that they worked for Mrs. Whitter, who runs a house on Old Pye Street."

Again, the urchin flinched away, but he was quick enough to snatch the half crown out of the air when Pinsley tossed it his way. He turned and ran. Pinsley let him go, trying to overrule his emotions. It was impossible not to feel fear for Kaia at the sound of that street, and worry at the sheer enormity of what he was going to have to do next.

It looked like he was going to have to find a way right into the heart of the Devil's Acre.

CHAPTER TWENTY SEVEN

Kaia kept trying to fight as they dragged her through the streets, to an area where the ground below their feet was somehow swampy with river water even in the midst of the city. Duckboards ran between islands of dry ground, and half the buildings around her had fallen in sections of roof or scorch marks from fires.

The whole place seemed dingy and at odds with the rest of Westminster, while Kaia thought she saw people looking out of tenements here and there, staring at her but making no move to help. They seemed like ghosts, too sickly looking and often dressed in rags. Here and there, she saw a more expensive piece of clothing, like a well-polished top hat or a silver topped cane, but they were so at odds with everything else there that it was obvious to her that they were stolen.

Kaia wasn't sure she'd ever been this afraid before. Not in the orphanage, not waiting in the cells to be dragged in front of the magistrate, not even in the church in the moments before she'd blown out all of its windows. Somehow, having had the power to do that before only made her feel more powerless now that the power wouldn't come.

It meant that she couldn't do anything as her two abductors more or less carried her in the direction of a gaudily painted tenement building at the heart of it all, two doors down from the noise of a gin palace. A couple of young women stood there in bright dresses and too much makeup, giving passersby bored looks.

Kaia might have been brought up isolated from the world in an orphanage, but she could still guess what this place was. She started to struggle again and one of the men carrying her struck her on the back of the head.

"Less of that. Mrs. Whitter won't give us the best price if you're fighting all the time, and she'll just have it beaten out of you."

They dragged her into the building, where the main room featured more women and bawdy, obviously drunk, men sitting on couches eying them. A piano was playing badly in the background, while the whole place stank of sweat and alcohol. A large, bald man with a scarred face took a look at Kaia and her captors before waving them through into a back room that had bare walls and peeling plaster on the ceiling. An old woman sat on a high backed chair, counting coins.

She wore a dress that wouldn't have suited her thirty years ago, let along now, while her hair was wispy and white, and she wore so much powder that it was hard to see any of the wrinkles beneath. She had a stick leaning against the table, and she took it up in one crabbed hand. Her eyes though, those were hard and hungry, scanning over Kaia like she was a side of meat to be bought at market.

"Now then, what have you brought for me?" she said, standing.

"A new girl for you, Mrs. Whitter," the Irishman who had helped grab Kaia said. "If the money's right."

"Oh, did you hear that Andrew?" the old woman said. "A new girl for you to try out. Well, let's see her."

Kaia could only stand there as her captors pulled the coat away from her. She looked round for a way out, but the big man who'd shown them in had shut a door behind her.

"Where'd you find her boys?" Mrs. Whitter asked. "That dress looks like quality. Wouldn't want *that* kind of trouble."

"Found her under a bridge, Mrs. Whitter," the other thug said. "Reckon she's a runaway."

Kaia couldn't believe they were talking about her as if she weren't even there. If there weren't a scarf stuffed into her mouth she might have screamed her anger at all of this.

"And no one finds runaways in the Devil's Acre," Mrs. Whitter said. "Hmm… pretty enough. Nice innocent look to her, and there's some who like that. How much?"

"Two guineas."

"Fifteen shillings, at most," Mrs. Whitter said.

"Thirty."

"One pound and that's an end to it."

"A guinea?"

"You're going to argue with me over an extra shilling?" Mrs. Witter said, and then laughed. "Oh, very well. I'll make it back from her on her first night."

She pushed a few coins across the table, and the men beside Kaia snatched them up quickly. The old woman came over to her, pulling the scarf out of her mouth.

"I'll never do what you want!" Kaia shouted at her. She would fight to her last breath. She would *find* a way to summon up the power that had helped her before. She would-

The old woman slapped her. "Oh, I do hope I haven't bruised you. Still, it's not your *face* men will care about. And you will do what I want, soon enough. Andrew, fetch the opium."

The big man went to a cupboard, taking out a vial. Kaia shied away from it, but the men holding Kaia kept her in place. The big man moved forward, and Mrs. Whitter smiled cruelly.

"No point fighting, dear. A little of this, and you'll soon see things our way," the old woman said. "Well, you'll be begging for more, at least, and *quite* willing to do what we want to earn it."

Kaia shut her mouth against the vial, shaking her head as the big man, Andrew, closed her nose. She held her breath, even though she knew it was hopeless. She would have to breathe sometime, but for now, at least, she had to *try* to fight.

Mrs. Whitter's helper, thug, whatever he was towered over Kaia, keeping his grip on her nose tight so that Kaia had to fight to keep from opening her mouth. As useless as it was, she kept her jaw clamped shut.

Then the sound of splintering wood came to Kaia's ears, and someone stepped past her, hitting the big man hard enough to send him sprawling. Kaia's eyes widened in shock as she recognized Inspector Pinsley. He was there? She couldn't believe that for a second, even as he stepped in, throwing a jab and a cross to the jaw of the bigger man as he started to get up again. Kaia almost cried out in joy as he slumped into unconsciousness.

"Don't just stand there," Mrs. Whitter said, and the two men holding Kaia let go of her, moving to circle Pinsley. Kaia felt sudden worry then, because she couldn't believe that even the inspector could fight two men at once.

"I should probably point out that I am a police inspector, madam," Pinsley said.

"You think that makes a difference, here?" Mrs. Whitter demanded. "We chase the police out of the Devil's Acre. That, or we throw them in the river. Get him, boys."

Kaia felt a moment of fear as the two thugs who had grabbed her went at Pinsley at once. He sidestepped them smoothly, though, and snatched the walking stick out of Mrs. Whitter's hands, bringing it up the way a fencer might hold a sword.

The Irishman ran at him, and Kaia gasped as Pinsley sidestepped the rush, striking him hard as he passed with the stick.

"Look out!" she called, and Pinsley barely turned in time to block a blow from the second of the kidnappers, striking him on the wrist hard enough to make him wince. A second blow caught him on the knee, buckling his leg.

The man came up, and now there was a knife in his hand. Instead of backing away, though, Pinsley threw the stick at his face, and then came in behind it with a chopping hook that felled his would-be attacker like a falling tree.

The Irishman was back in the fight, though. He grabbed Pinsley, and Kaia thought that the inspector was done for, except he somehow managed to step to one side and fling his attacker off him, throwing him to the ground hard enough that the man could only lie there, groaning.

"You think I'm just going to let you out of here?" Mrs. Whitter demanded. She had a knife of her own now, which she brandished, catching the light.

"Yes, madam," Pinsley said. "I think you are."

He withdrew something from one of his pockets. Kaia realized to her shock that it was a pistol.

"My superintendent does not like his officers to carry guns," he said. "At best, he agreed to a few aged flintlocks. Thankfully, I do not have to worry about such things at the moment. This is a Beaumont-Adams .442 revolver, a souvenir from my time in the Crimean Peninsula. If you give me cause to use it, I promise we will all regret it. Kaia, are you all right?"

"They haven't hurt me yet," Kaia said, trying not to let too much of her fear show. She was more grateful than she could have imagined that Pinsley was there. "Can you untie me?"

He edged back to her, untying her one handed while keeping his eyes on Mrs. Whitter. The big, bald man was starting to stir, and Kaia hoped that Pinsley would hurry up. Finally though, the scarves fell away from her, leaving her free.

"You won't get far!" Mrs. Whitter promised.

"Far enough, I think," Pinsley said, and raised the pistol towards the ceiling, pulling the trigger.

The bang of it was enough to deafen Kaia, but then Pinsley was pulling at her arm, dragging her out of there. Around her, women were screaming and running, trying to get out of the house. Lost in the midst

140

of them, she and Pinsley hurried out into the street. There was shouting behind them, but they kept running, not stopping until the swampiness of the Devil's Acre gave way to the firmer ground and finer buildings of the rest of Westminster.

"You came for me," Kaia said, when they finally came to a halt. She wasn't sure whether to be grateful or shocked right then. "You saved me."

"I should never have let the constables try to take you," Pinsley said. Kaia suspected that it was the closest thing to an apology she was going to hear from the inspector. They kept walking, hurrying through the streets of London, putting more distance between them and everything that had just happened.

"Where are we going?" Kaia asked.

"I'm not sure yet," Pinsley said. "I still need to think. But I know now that you're a part of this. I saw what you did with the constables. I can't quite *believe* what you did, but I still saw it. There is something bigger here than I imagined."

"How much bigger?" Kaia asked.

"That is the part that I still need to think about," Pinsley said. He took something else out of his pocket, and Kaia didn't realize what it was until the inspector set the metronome on a wall and started it ticking, chopping up the world with a regular pulse.

"What is that for," Kaia asked.

"It helps me think," Pinsley said. "I am sure that we have all the pieces of this. The murder, the log book... wait, the log book."

"What about it?" Kaia asked. "There was no one in it. We checked it, and every other bit of paper in Bedlam."

"That's the *point*," Pinsley said. "There was another visitor earlier, for another patient, an Agatha Simpkins. But..." He put his hands to his head as if he might be able to drag the memory of it out by force. "Yes, I'm sure of it. The papers we looked at before I got so caught up with the keeper included transfer papers for that patient, two days beforehand. A transfer to Harrogate. Stupid. How could I have been so stupid as to have missed this?"

Stupid? He thought it was stupid to miss a connection between two documents he'd only seen briefly, and was piecing together from memory? Kaia couldn't imagine anyone else doing it.

"That's... incredible," she said, marveling at the ease with which the inspector had pieced that together. "But what does it mean?"

"It means that someone else went into Bedlam that day," Pinsley said. "It means that we have a way that Tabitha could have been killed. A killer went in, pretending to visit a prisoner, waited, and then killed her later. He gave the name…" Pinsley concentrated for a second. "John Smith when he visited. If we find out who that was, we'll have our killer."

The sound of applause came to Kaia through the London night. A tall figure stepped into the edge of the light spread by a gas lamp, and it took Kaia a moment to recognize Doctor de Vere.

"Very good, Inspector," he said. He held out a hand, and a surgeon's knife glinted in it. "Just as it is impressive that you have found the girl even before I could. Still, things must come to an end. Hand her over, or I'm afraid to say that I will have to kill you both."

CHAPTER TWENTY EIGHT

Kaia stared at Doctor de Vere as he stood there in the half light of the street lamp. She could feel the sense of wrongness building up in her as she looked at him, could feel that mix of fear, revulsion and the simple sense that something about him was barely even human.

Around him, the shadows of the streetlight danced, forming patterns that might have been taken as a trick of the light by anyone else. Kaia knew better now, though. She didn't know what was going on, but she knew those dancing shadows were something real, something dangerous.

They wreathed Doctor de Vere as he pointed his knife at her again, the sight of him there making her shudder.

"I'll ask again," he said to Inspector Pinsley. "Give me the girl. She is the one who is relevant here. You... you don't even matter."

"Why?" Kaia asked. She saw a chance to finally get the truth of this, and she knew that she couldn't pass that chance up, no matter how frightened she felt. "What's going on here? What's all this about?"

"Even now, you don't understand," Doctor de Vere said. "You wear the mark of the shadow-seers, like her, and you understand as little of what's going on. I could put you in Bedlam, and they'd just think you were mad."

"Making it easy for you to come and kill Kaia, the way you did Tabitha Greene," Pinsley said. "I know what you did. I know they would have made you sign in, so you used a false name, and pretended to visit a different prisoner."

"Ah, you were doing so well," Doctor de Vere said. "You still haven't seen the part where there's someone else involved in this. I am not your John Smith. I had no *need* to kill Tabitha Greene, when she was shut away. And if you, girl had not run, I would have no need to kill you either."

Kaia wasn't sure that she believed that. She couldn't believe anything that she heard coming out of the doctor's mouth. Even so, there was something about the denial that made her pause.

Apparently, it was enough to make Pinsley pause as well.

"If not you, then who?" the inspector said. Kaia saw his hand creeping towards his pocket, and she remembered the revolver from before. She would feel a lot safer around the doctor's knife once he had the gun out and aimed.

"I will make a deal with you, Inspector," Doctor de Vere said. He lowered the knife, but Kaia didn't believe for a moment that it meant the threat was gone. "Hand over the girl, and I will tell you who your 'John Smith' is. I will tell you where to find the killer."

"I'm not giving you Kaia," Pinsley said.

"No? But the killer is what you want, isn't it?" the doctor said. "What use is this girl to you? Has she helped you at any point, really?"

Kaia started to worry then, because Pinsley had already made it clear just how little she'd helped him.

"Whereas I can help you to find the truth," the doctor went on. "It's a simple trade, Inspector. Give her to me, and you get everything you've been looking for. You'll have your precious answers, and those might even be enough to get you your position back."

"And in return, all I have to do is give you Kaia?" Pinsley said.

"No," Kaia said, suddenly terrified that he might actually do it. "You can't."

"No," the inspector agreed. "I can't, and I won't. You, Doctor, are guilty of abusing your position at the very least. I am not putting Kaia in danger by handing her to you."

"*Give* her to me!" the doctor snarled, lifting his blade again. He charged with the weapon raised.

"Watch out!" Kaia yelled, but Pinsley was already pulling his revolver from his pocket. He fired, but the shadows around the doctor seemed to swirl, the shot went wide, and then Doctor de Vere was slamming into him. The gun went spinning across the cobbles, and Kaia saw the knife come up.

The two men grappled over the knife, striking at one another as they fought. Kaia had seen the inspector fight before, but the doctor seemed stronger than a slender man like him should have been, and the knife made him far more dangerous. Kaia didn't want to think about what might happen if the doctor succeeded in getting his knife arm free, even for a moment.

They battered at one another, wrestling to break one another's grips while Kaia tried to work out what she could do to help. She saw Pinsley hit the doctor with a hard hook to the body that looked as if it should have doubled up most men, but the doctor kept fighting. The

144

two of them went down in a tangle together, rolling over and over as they fought.

Kaia grabbed for the revolver, lifting it and aiming it as best she could, trying to work out if she could bring herself to pull the trigger, even in the midst of such a deadly struggle. She realized that there was a bigger problem than that, though, because there was no way that she could get a clear shot at the doctor with the two of them grappling so close.

She realized that there was something she *could* do, though. Setting the gun aside, Kaia rushed in instead, grabbing for the doctor's knife arm. She succeeded in getting a grip with both hands, clinging on as best she could, even while the doctor thrashed to get clear.

"I'll kill you both!" the doctor yelled.

Even as he did it, the inspector seemed to realize the opportunity that Kaia was giving him. He let go of the doctor's knife arm, rearing back.

For a moment, Kaia was sure that she'd made a mistake, and that she wouldn't be able to keep her grip. She was sure that the doctor was going to break free, and then they would both die.

Then the inspector slammed a punch forward into the doctor's jaw once, then again. This close, Kaia could hear the sound of the impact. She felt the moment when the doctor slumped to the ground unconscious, and heard the clatter of the knife falling to the ground.

"Are you all right?" Pinsley asked her, helping her to her feet.

"I'm fine," Kaia assured him, although she could hear the shake in her own voice as she did it. When the doctor had been attacking, there hadn't been time to be terrified by it all, but now there was more than enough time to be afraid. Kaia felt the tremors spreading through her body.

"It's all right," Pinsley said, putting a hand on her shoulder. "It's done. We stopped him."

He went over to pick up his gun.

"How did you miss him before?" Kaia asked. "I thought you were in the army."

"I was," the inspector said. "But even there, I was never a terribly good shot."

"Not terribly good?" Kaia said. At that range even not terribly good should have been more than enough to hit.

"Well, truth be told, I was a famously *bad* shot," the inspector said. He looked a little embarrassed. "Although even I should have been able to hit at that range. It seemed to me almost as if... as if..."

Kaia waited for him to finish, hoping that he would understand the way the shadows had moved to distract him. Instead, to her frustration, the inspector shook his head.

"That doesn't matter now. What matters is..." Kaia could see him looking down at the doctor, shaking his head. "He attacked us. He wanted *you*."

Kaia saw him looking at the doctor, obviously trying to calculate how all this fit together. For her part, the main thing that Kaia felt was gratitude.

"You didn't hand me over to him," she said.

The inspector looked surprised. "I would never do that, Kaia. I hope you believe me when I say that."

To her surprise Kaia found that she *did* believe him, and that was enough to make tears well up in her eyes.

"What is it?" Pinsley said. "Kaia, are you all right?"

"Yes," she said. "It's just... no one has ever cared before. And I've... you could have found out who did this."

"I'll get the information out of him when he wakes up," Pinsley assured her.

Kaia didn't think that was likely, though. The doctor had seemed determined, and he was good at manipulating things too. What could the detective do? Drag him back to the police station? His bosses would probably let the doctor go, and send her straight to Bedlam, the way they'd tried to before. They weren't going to be able to just get information from him. The inspector had given that possibility away the moment he'd refused to hand her over.

And he'd still done it.

"I still can't believe that he attacked us like this," Pinsley said, looking down at the doctor. "If he's serious about not having killed Tabitha Greene, then why would he have done something like this? It makes no sense. And why attack us like some madman? I know he was an addict, but this... and what's this about 'shadowseers?'"

Kaia wished that she had an answer for him. Instead, she found her eyes drawn to the spot where the doctor lay, still unconscious from the inspector's blows. She started as she thought she saw him begin to stir, and wondered if she should alert the inspector.

Then she saw that it wasn't the doctor stirring at all, it was the shadows around him. They writhed like snakes, and his body seemed almost to convulse on the ground. His mouth opened wide, and something seemed to pour from him. Kaia gasped in shock as shadows flowed out of him like dark water, unable to believe that something like that had been in him all along. She could feel the wrongness of those shadows, the dangerous power of them, and the sight of them there scared her.

Then they were off, slithering from patch of darkness to patch of darkness, never spending more than a moment or two in the light. It was as if, outside the doctor's body, the light hurt them. The shadows should have been invisible in the darkness, but now that she had seen them, Kaia found her eyes fixed on them.

The shadows sped out away from Kaia, and a part of her wanted to just let them go. This wasn't over, though, and Kaia was certain of one thing: they weren't fleeing at random. They were heading somewhere, and Kaia didn't know where, but she also knew that she couldn't let this go. Without even pausing to try to explain things to the inspector, she set off after the shadows.

"Kaia, where are you going?" Pinsley called after her.

Kaia didn't slow down. She kept running, keeping her eyes fixed to the shadows so that she wouldn't lose them. She heard Pinsley's footsteps following hers, but even if he hadn't followed, she would have kept running. She was certain now: following the shadows was the only way they were going to get answers.

CHAPTER TWENTY NINE

Kaia raced across London, desperate to keep up with the shadows ahead of her. She didn't know what was happening, but if she slowed down now, she was sure that she would never find an answer.

"Kaia, stop!" Pinsley shouted after her. "What are you doing?"

He couldn't see it, Kaia realized. The shadows were there, flowing like dark water across the streets, moving from patch of darkness to patch of darkness, completely obvious to her. Yet the inspector was shouting after her like he couldn't see any of them.

"Kaia, slow down!" Pinsley shouted. "We can't just leave the doctor!"

Kaia could still hear his footsteps following, though. She hoped that she was leading him the right way. There was still the worry at the back of her mind that she might be seeing things. If she was seeing racing shadows and the inspector couldn't, what did that mean? Kaia didn't know, but she was sure that this meant something. There were answers here, if only she could keep up.

They seemed to be heading north, following the curve of the Thames for the moment. Kaia ran down the center of the street, and if this had been the day, she would have been run over by a cart or a carriage in seconds. Even at night, she had to dodge out of the way of a hansom cab, but didn't let that slow her down.

"Kaia, you're going to be hurt!" Pinsley called after her.

Kaia kept dodging through the London night. She pushed past a couple walking out along the river, hitched her skirts up slightly, and kept running. She wasn't sure where she was now, but it seemed as if she'd gone through Westminster and out into somewhere else.

There were more people around, with brightly painted and lamp lit buildings that seemed to be theatres or drinking establishments. Kaia realized that she'd been there with Pinsley before, passing through this space on the way out towards Camden. This was Soho, wasn't it?

Kaia didn't know for sure, and she didn't care, right then. The only thing that mattered was trying to keep up with the shadows. That was far from easy, because untethered from a body, they were fast.

They idea that these shadows might have been in the doctor, filling him and maybe even controlling him, was a hard one to make sense of, yet Kaia couldn't think of another explanation.

"Kaia…" Pinsley grabbed her shoulder, and for a moment, Kaia had to spin to face him. He was looking at her with obvious concern, his breath coming raggedly. "What is this? What are you doing?"

"I need you to trust me," Kaia said, looking around. She panicked for a moment, because she'd lost sight of the shadows. They'd flitted away into the dark. She thought that she'd lost her chance. Despair filled her at the thought that she'd thrown away the chance to find the truth of all this.

Then she spotted something moving again, and caught sight of the shadows flashing forward in the distance. Kaia pulled away from Pinsley, and set off running once more, in the direction the shadows had gone.

"Where are we going?" the inspector asked.

"This way!" Kaia called out, and kept following the shadows. There was a busy street ahead, with more people on it than Kaia might have expected for a city street at night. This part of London, though, seemed to be somewhere that didn't sleep, with the lights of the lamps spilling out to dispel the darkness around.

Kaia saw the shadows flowing through that space, twisting and turning to avoid the worst of the light. Again, she had the impression that they were hurt by that light when they stayed in it too long. She kept following, pushing her way through the crowds there.

It was hard to keep her eyes on the shadows as she pushed her way through the crowds on the streets. She didn't slow down, though, not now. If anything, Kaia felt that she was starting to catch up, now that the shadows were having to take a more circuitous path.

They darted down an alley, and Kaia followed, a few paces ahead of the inspector as he still struggled to break free of the crowds. There weren't people here, because there were no entertainments to tempt them. The alleyway was darker as a result, but Kaia didn't find that slowing her down.

Then shadows reared up in the darkness in front of her, lunging towards Kaia like a striking snake. Too late, she realized that the shadows had been moving slower for a reason, luring her closer step by step until she was near enough for them to strike at her.

They washed over her, wrapping around her so that the whole world seemed like it was covered in a gauzy haze of shadows. The world around Kaia seemed to be filled with whispers as the shadows tried to force their way into her mouth, her nose, her ears.

Give in. Yield to us. Humanity is a curse upon the world...

"No!" Kaia cried out, and the shadows fell back from her. They couldn't get in. They couldn't control her. That realization filled Kaia with relief, but even so, she knew the danger wasn't done here.

She grabbed for the shadows, but they felt insubstantial under Kaia's grasp. It was like trying to grab smoke. They didn't seem to be able to touch her either. If they could, she had no doubt that they would have wrapped around her throat to strangle her, or torn her apart with shards of darkness.

She realized then what that meant. The shadows needed to be in someone to hurt or kill. *That* was why there had been someone else in Bedlam, because the shadows couldn't strike at Tabitha directly.

That still didn't tell her who they'd been in, but Kaia had the feeling that after being driven out of the doctor, these shadows were looking for somewhere they knew. They could have tried to get into any of the people of London, but instead, it seemed that they were going somewhere specific.

Kaia wished that she knew where. For the moment, though, it seemed that she was stuck trying to follow in the wake of the shadows, which raced along now, barely giving her any chance to keep up. Kaia's heart pounded as she ran, taking corners as fast as her hooped skirts would allow, determined not to let the shadows out of her sight.

She almost found herself knocked flat by a party of revelers out in Soho, wealthy young men by the look of them, maybe out there from the universities, or visiting town specifically for the entertainments. Kaia managed to regain her balance, but one of them caught her wrist.

"Why are you in such a hurry to run off?" he asked. "I'm sure we could show you a great time."

"Let go of me," Kaia said.

"Oh, don't be so coy," the young man said. "Why don't we-"

"Let go of her unless you want to see the inside of a police cell," Pinsley said, as he caught up. Kaia found herself grateful once again that she had the inspector on her side. This was the third time in one night that he'd saved her.

"No need to make a fuss about it," the student said, and he and his friends moved off in search of the next source of amusement.

That left Kaia looking round, trying to find the direction the shadows had gone.

"What is all this about, Kaia?" Pinsley asked.

"I thought…" Kaia tried to think of a way to put this that would satisfy his need for a rational explanation for all of this. "Does it make sense if I say that I saw something that I followed this way? That I have a feeling that I think can lead us to the killer?"

"I'm not sure," the inspector admitted, but it was certainly better than the ways he'd reacted before. "What I saw you do before seems impossible, but you *did* it. If you can lead me to the killer, I'm not going to question how you've done that. *Can* you find the killer?"

Kaia looked around, trying to find the shadows again, but the trail had gone cold. The shadows had disappeared, taking the opportunity to get away while she was distracted.

She could still feel that pulsing sense of wrongness that she'd gotten from the doctor, and from Bedlam, though. It was like a pull on the edges of her mind, and Kaia found that if she took careful steps, she could tell where the feeling of something wrong was stronger and where it faded almost to nothingness. It was like listening in to some faint sound, trying to find the place where it was clearest.

Kaia walked back and forth, trying to pin it down. It was hard to find, but Kaia found that if she concentrated, she could keep the sense of it clear in her head. She paced slowly along the street, feeling the sensation get stronger and stronger as she walked along a row of houses. When it started to grow fainter again, Kaia stopped and walked back again.

Again, it grew stronger, and then fainter. Kaia stopped at the point where it was strongest, looking around and trying to make some sense of it. There was a wrought iron gateway there, and beyond it, there seemed to be steps, leading down below the level of the street. There were statues to either side, although their faces had been broken off by someone.

"What is this?" Kaia asked the inspector. He seemed to know every part of London, so perhaps he knew what was down those steps.

"I think this used to be some kind of religious house," Pinsley said. "Although it doesn't seem to be currently in use. If it was Catholic, there is a chance that it was damaged or destroyed in the riots seventy years ago. A lot of Soho was damaged."

Why would the shadows run to some old religious building? Kaia didn't know, but now that she was standing in front of the steps, she was certain that the sense of wrongness that she felt was emanating from down there. She tried the iron gate and was surprised to find that it was unlocked. Kaia swung it open slowly, staring down into the dark.

"Down there?" Pinsley asked. "You think the killer is down there?"

Kaia nodded. She couldn't be certain based on just a feeling, but there was only one way to find out. With the inspector in her wake, she started off down the steps.

CHAPTER THIRTY

Pinsley tried to make sense of the chase Kaia had just led him on, across half of London. She seemed so certain that this was where they had to go, and yet Pinsley couldn't see the reason behind it, the logic, the purpose of all this.

That scared him, more than a little; acting without reason was dangerously close to chaos. Yet he also found himself trusting Kaia, and her instincts. If she said that this was the place where answers were to be found, then Pinsley was willing to at least look.

He led the way down the steps, into the ruins of the old chapel.

Pinsley had half expected to have to strike a match just to be able to see down there, but as it was the packet of lucifers in his pocket went untouched. There was more than enough light coming in through the chapel's windows from street lamps beyond. To his surprise, there were candles burning too, dribbling in sconces and candelabra that looked as if they'd been taken from multiple different places.

Pinsley frowned at that and looked over to Kaia. He put a finger to his lips. Someone needed to have lit the candles, and that someone might still be there. He saw Kaia nod, padding along in his wake.

The inspector could feel his blood pumping now, his belief in Kaia rising. He still didn't know how she'd brought them to this place, but all his faculties told him that they were nearing the end of this.

The space at the foot of the stairs was... unusual. Most of it was what Pinsley might have expected. It had a vaulted ceiling, held up by solid limestone pillars. There were partially repainted frescoes on the walls that appeared to show saints, and statues of them set in niches. Pinsley recognized the symbolism for St Dymphna, patron saint of the insane, St Lucy, patron of those who could not see, Bernard of Clairvaux, who was associated with chandlers and monks...

The strange part was that those statues didn't quite fit with one another. Nor did the candle holders or the few pieces of furniture in there. Even the paintings on the walls looked like they'd been taken from a dozen different places. Pinsley could see the scorch marks beneath, and the chipped stone where things had been attacked with a

153

hammer, sometime in the distant past. He ran a hand along one of the walls, trying to make sense of it.

"Here," Kaia whispered over to him, and he went to the spot where she stood. There, in the shadow of one of the pillars, there was a collection of blankets.

"Someone has been living down here," Pinsley whispered. He felt almost eager, like a fisherman who had finally gotten a bite on the line. Of course, London had many homeless, but this wasn't just that, he was sure of it.

Kaia nodded. She looked almost as eager as Pinsley felt. He needed to find the truth of this, and this was where Kaia had led him. There were answers there, if only he could find them.

He looked round another pillar, and saw the start of them. The square stone block of the altar stood there, with candle after candle set upon it. A figure knelt in front of it, and for a moment Pinsley thought that he was praying, whispering there and seeking redemption.

That didn't seem quite right, though. This was about more than that. Pinsley looked at him closely. He was hunched over, but the inspector guessed that he would have been a large man standing up. His hair was shaggy and unkempt, while he had a beard that looked like it hadn't been trimmed in a while. He wore all black, including a long, dark coat that spread out across the floor like a pool of dark water.

"A shadow," Pinsley whispered, understanding dawning. *This* was why Elsie had spoken over and over about a shadow killing Tabitha Greene. It had been a man wrapped in black, with no supernatural explanation to it at all. He almost laughed at the simplicity of it. However she had done it, Kaia had led him to the truth of this.

"Stay behind the pillars," Pinsley whispered to her, taking out his revolver once again.

"What happened to you being a famously bad shot?" Kaia asked.

"*He* doesn't know that," Pinsley said.

Kaia did as he asked, siding into place behind one of the pillars there, even if Pinsley could see her peeking out, making sure that she could still see.

On silent feet, Pinsley padded towards his quarry.

*

Kaia stayed almost frozen in place, watching the inspector start to advance on the figure kneeling there. When the man spoke, she all but jumped out of her skin.

"This was a holy place once," the man kneeling there said. "It was destroyed years ago, but never deconsecrated. I thought that if I put it back together, I might be able to put myself back together, too. I lit candles, to keep the shadows out, but it's not enough. It's never enough."

He stood up and turned. Kaia could see how gaunt he was, how pale and shaky.

"Opium?" Pinsley said. Kaia was surprised that he would confront him about it like that.

"I was… weak," the man said. "I knew that someone would come for me eventually, you know."

"After you used a fake name to get into Bedlam, John Smith?" Pinsley said.

"Xander," the man said. "My name is Xander."

"But I'm right about the rest, aren't I?" Pinsley said. "You pretended to visit another inmate there, but you used the chance to get to Tabitha Greene."

"I didn't want to kill her," the man said.

To Kaia, he sounded as if he meant it. She didn't know what to make of that. All the time, she could feel that sense of wrongness pervading this place. Some of it came from the man in front of her, but more of it, far more, was off in the darkness beyond the candles.

"But you did?" Pinsley said.

Xander took out something metal and rake like that fit into the palm of his hand. The points of it were sharp as razors, catching the light.

"I used this," he said. "You should arrest me. I thought that I could overcome my weaknesses, but I can't. It isn't safe for me to be out in the world."

"You're giving yourself up?" Pinsley asked. Kaia noted that his revolver never left the man in front of him.

She couldn't blame him for that. If this was the man who had killed Tabitha, then there was every chance that he was dangerous. Yet there was something else about him, too, something haunted, something that made Kaia want to have sympathy for him in spite of what he'd done.

"If I'm not stopped, the shadows will come again," the man said. "We see them, we fight them, but I was weak. I took laudanum for my wounds, and then… I couldn't stop."

155

Kaia saw the inspector take another step towards him, gun still outstretched. Kaia knew that she ought to just stay there and let him complete the arrest, but if he did, would this moment ever come again? She found herself thinking of what the doctor had called her before the shadows had poured out of him. She knew that she had to have an answer, even if it meant not doing what the inspector had told her.

"What is a shadow-seer?" Kaia asked him, stepping out from the shelter of the pillar that she had hidden behind. "Do you know? Are you one?"

He'd talked about seeing shadows, after all. It wasn't such a big leap to think that he might be the same as Kaia, and Tabitha. If so, did that mean that there were more of them?

He stared at her. "You... yes, I am a shadow-seer. I was one of them, at least, until my need for opium grew too great. They cast me beyond their ranks then, said that I could not be trusted to keep the shadows from within me." He clutched at his head, as if the memory of it hurt him.

"Kaia, I told you to stay out of sight," Pinsley said. "It isn't safe."

"It isn't," Xander said. "I thought it was safe, with Tabitha. I thought I could help her. She didn't know what she was, or what it meant. I thought... I thought I could bring her to the others, and they would forgive me. I thought if I could bring another shadow-seer to them, I could show that I was still strong. But that place! You've felt that place?"

Kaia nodded. She'd felt what Bedlam was like. Every moment, it pressed in, and there was a darkness there that felt more than simply the effects of so much madness so close by.

She wasn't sure how much she dared to say then. She wanted to know more about shadow-seers, but if she said too much, would it just spook this man who was obviously hanging onto sanity by a thread?

"What is a shadow-seer?" Kaia asked. "A man used that word about me."

"Kaia," Pinsley said. "The murder..."

"You're a shadow-seer?" Xander said. He stared at Kaia, and it seemed to her that a look of recognition dawned on him. "Yes, I see it. Just like she was. You look just like her."

"Tabitha?" Kaia said. She didn't think that she looked anything like Tabitha, except for the mark on her arm.

"No," Xander replied. "Your mother."

Those words made it feel as though the world came to a sudden, jarring stop. This man knew something about her mother? He'd said it with a certainty that left no room for doubt, as if it were simply obvious who Kaia' mother was.

"Kaia, you can't listen to anything this man says," Pinsley said. "He's saying whatever he can to-"

"To what?" Kaia countered. "He's already confessed to murdering Tabitha."

"That was the shadow in me," Xander said. "I was too weak to resist. I couldn't stop it."

"And the church? Was it you attacking Reverend Faulkner?"

Xander shook his head, though, which left Kaia puzzled. Did that mean that the shadows had taken control of someone else? The threat of them striking with anyone in London who was weakened enough to let them in was terrifying.

In spite of everything, Kaia found herself believing Xander. She'd seen the way the shadows had poured out of the doctor, so was it so hard to believe that more might have found their way into this man? Right then, though, there was only one thing she wanted to know.

"Tell me about my mother," she said. "Who was she? Did you know her? Was she a shadow-seer?"

"Kaia, I know you have questions," Pinsley said, "but we need to bring this man in first."

"I'll come quietly," Xander said. "I'll tell you anything you want about the murder, and about your mother, young lady. She was-"

He didn't finish that, though, because that was the moment when Kaia saw shadows rise up behind him like a predator preparing to strike at its prey.

"Look out!" she yelled, and Xander spun towards the threat, crying out in obvious fear. She saw Pinsley staring blankly, as if he couldn't see what the two of them saw.

Kaia could see the moment when the shadows attacked, though, washing over Xander the way they'd washed over her before. Then, they hadn't been able to find a way inside her, but with Xander, they poured in as if he were some empty cup they were filling to the brim. He spasmed with his arms out wide, his whole body going rigid as he tried to fight, but it made no difference.

Kaia felt the wrongness in him, felt the presence of the shadows as surely as she had with the doctor. He turned back towards her and Pinsley, lifting the metal claws that he'd fashioned.

"Stop!" The inspector called out. "Stop, or I will shoot!"

"Time to die, girl," Xander said, and although it was the same voice, there was something colder about it and more dangerous. "Time to join dear Tabitha in the grave."

He leapt at them with all the fury of some inhuman beast.

CHAPTER THIRTY ONE

"Watch out!" Kaia yelled, because she knew that the inspector couldn't see what she did. "He's going to-"

She was too slow, and saw Xander lash out at Pinsley, slashing at him with the sharpened, claw like hand rake. Kaia flinched as the inspector cried out, not wanting him to be hurt.

The gun went off, but all it meant was that a statuette nearby shattered as Pinsley's shot hit it rather than his foe. Kaia saw Xander slam a backhanded strike into the inspector's wrist, sending the gun spinning away beyond the circle of the candles.

Pinsley and Xander circled one another. The inspector had a slash across his overcoat now, and there were splatters of blood against the shine of Xander's blades. Kaia hated the sight of that, and hated the fact that she was just standing there watching it even more.

She wasn't going to be some helpless girl standing there while the two men fought. She'd helped in the fight against the doctor, after all. She waited while Pinsley threw a couple of punches in Xander's direction, forcing the other man back. He slashed back at the inspector, and Pinsley gave ground in turn.

Kaia watched them play cat and mouse with one another, each of them looking for an opening to strike at the other. Kaia might not be an expert on fighting, but she could see that Xander was much better at it than Doctor de Vere had been. He knew how to use the slashing claws of the hand rake he held, although the shortness of its spikes meant that he couldn't just stand off and slash the inspector to shreds.

Instead, the two of them had to probe for weaknesses. The inspector had his hands up like a prize fighter, constantly moving, seemingly looking for a chance to land a knockout blow. Xander, meanwhile, was weaving his weapon back and forth, making it impossible for Pinsley to grab at his arm without getting cut.

This time, Kaia didn't feel as if she could dive into the middle of it all, but she *could* try to distract Xander at least. Maybe she could even stop all this. He was only fighting because of the shadow inside him,

159

after all, its presence pressing in on Kaia's mind, making her want to back away.

"Xander, fight it," she said. "If you're like me, then you have the strength to keep it out."

"He has no power anymore," Xander, or the shadow within him, said. "I don't even have to pretend that he is in control. He is weak, and soon, you will be dead."

He slashed out at the inspector, then, as Pinsley dodged the attack, he swung towards Kaia and lunged at her. Kaia threw herself to the side as he slashed at her, tripped and rolled. Too late, she saw more of the candles set out there on the floor, and her dress smoldered as she scrambled to her feet. Kaia stamped on the hem, struggling to put out the flames before they burnt her.

Xander came at her again, but this time the inspector was there, moving between them. He held a tall candelabrum now, holding it like a spear with a flaming head and jabbing it at his opponent so that the other man barely managed to parry it. He slashed back, and Kaia heard Pinsley cry out as the blades cut into his arm.

"Get the gun," Pinsley called to Kaia, without looking round. The candles in his improvised weapon left light trails as he kept it between him and Xander.

"We can't shoot him," Kaia said, even though she could feel the fear of the shadow within their attacker almost overwhelming her now.

"I know we need him alive to arrest him," Pinsley said. "But-"

"You think you're going to arrest me?" Xander said. "I'm not the one bleeding, Inspector."

He lunged at Pinsley again, but the inspector managed to tangle his legs with the candelabrum, tripping him. Kaia took the chance to break away from the two of them, moving out through the underground chapel, trying to work out the best way to help with this.

Should she try to find the gun? Kaia didn't want to, and not just because of how impossible it had been to use in the fight against the doctor. The inspector still seemed to be thinking in terms of a foe who could be threatened into stillness, who might behave rationally if Kaia managed to get a weapon pointed at him. She had seen the shadows pour into him, though, and she knew what she was dealing with. Those shadows didn't care if the man under their control lived or died. If she had the gun, then she would have to kill Xander with it, and Kaia wasn't sure that she could bring herself to kill someone.

It wasn't just that, though. It was also the thought that, if she did, she would never get answers. He knew about her mother, and about what it meant to be the "shadow-seer" the doctor had called her. She needed him alive, and so did the inspector, because who was going to believe that this was the real killer without his confession. She couldn't just kill him.

That left Kaia looking around for something that might help her and the inspector to win without having to kill Xander outright. She hunted around until she found a statue that looked as if it might be heavy enough to knock out the large, shaggy haired figure of the former shadow-seer. She hefted it and started forward, hoping that she could sneak up behind Xander and bring an end to all of this.

Kaia padded forward, determined to make no sound. She had to force herself to move forward, because the overwhelming sense of the shadow there in Xander was almost enough to push her back from him. She tiptoed towards him, picking her way closer, step by step.

Somehow though, Xander knew that she was coming, because he spun towards her, swiping at her with his weapon with brutal speed. Kaia managed to get the statuette she held in the way, barely, but the impact was still enough to shatter it. She took a step back, managing to avoid another swipe, and then the inspector was there between them.

Xander hit him, and Kaia cried out as she saw the inspector crumple beneath the blow, flung back hard enough for his head to slam against a column while blood covered his chest. Was he hurt, unconscious, dead?

To Kaia's surprise, the possessed shadow-seer didn't press forward to finish his attack on her, not yet. Instead, he stood over the inspector, lifting his bloody weapon.

"I want you to know that you did this," he said. "You brought him here, following where you shouldn't. You got him hurt, too, interfering. I want you to know that, and I want you to watch him die before I kill you."

The worst part was that Kaia knew it was true. They'd only found this place because she'd been able to follow the shadows. The inspector had only thought that there was more to this at all because the two of them had investigated together. Looking down at the fallen form of the inspector, Kaia felt guilt that she'd brought him here, but also fear for what was going to happen next.

She couldn't hope to save the inspector. She couldn't even save herself. Even if she ran, there was no chance of her getting away before

Xander got to her. He'd already shown that there was no way to convince him to fight back against the shadows.

She was going to end up the way Tabitha had. Kaia had seen her body lying there on a slab, under the knife of the surgeon examining her. Was *she* going to be like that, just a thing to be examined? Was the inspector?

Kaia could feel the fear building up inside her as Xander started to crouch over the inspector. He lifted his hand rake, and Kaia knew that the next movement he made would see it plunging down into Pinsley's throat.

She felt something else building up inside her too, and Kaia realized that the same power that had come to her before was running through her. It felt as if it was filling her to bursting point, ready to spill out from her. Yet last time, when she'd thrown the police constables away from her, they'd been in contact with her. Did she need to touch Xander in order for this to work? Not knowing what else to do, she ran at Xander, ignoring her fear.

He looked up as she came at him, and some kind of realization seemed to dawn on his face as he looked at her, like he could see the buildup of power within her. He swung his homemade weapon at Kaia as if he might be able to stop her, but Kaia was moving too fast for that. She ran inside the arc of his attack, reaching out for him. She felt the breeze of the weapon passing close to her head, but there was no time to even think about the damage that could have done to her.

Instead, Kaia put her hand on Xander's chest, directly above the spot where the big man's heart lay.

Power pulsed out from Kaia in light and force so great that it seemed impossible that she had ever contained it. She felt the recoil of that power make her feet scrape back along the floor, but it was Xander the power really moved. Kaia saw him fly back from her, flung through the air like a kite in a strong wind, to land with a crack against one of the pillars there.

He slid down it, the hand rake clattering from his grip. He lay there, and his body seemed to writhe with shadows just beneath the skin. Then his mouth opened wide and he screamed, the sound seeming impossibly loud to Kaia in such an enclosed space.

Shadows flowed out from him as he screamed, billowing towards the roof of the chapel and swirling there like some great dark cloud. They flowed towards Kaia in a rush, but she stood there before them with her hand still outstretched, not giving ground. They flowed around

162

her and past her, moving on towards the gate leading out. It poured through that gate, the shadows seeming to join with the darkness beyond.

In just seconds, the shadows were gone, leaving Kaia panting as she stood there. Xander was groaning against the pillar where he'd fallen, and Pinsley… he lay on the ground, not moving.

"No!" Kaia cried out, running to him.

CHAPTER THIRTY TWO

Kaia stared down at Pinsley, not knowing what to do, or think. Was he hurt? Was he dead? No, he couldn't be. Kaia wouldn't be able to stand it if he was dead. The inspector had been the one to pluck her out from the police station, the one to give her somewhere to live, and to make her feel like she could do something valuable in the world. After all that, he couldn't be dead, he couldn't.

The shadows were gone, but she still had to find a way to help the inspector.

Kaia looked over his wounds, tearing open his overcoat and the waistcoat beneath to see blood staining the white of his shirt where Xander had slashed at him. The sheer amount of blood looked awful, and Kaia felt worry and grief building up in her. She'd lost everyone in her life. She couldn't lose the inspector too, not like this.

Then Pinsley gasped, his eyes coming open. He looked around as if searching for threats, and started to push to his feet.

"It's all right," Kaia said. "It's over."

The relief she felt as the inspector stood was immense. He looked over to where Xander lay as if wanting to verify that for himself.

"Are you all right?" Pinsley asked. "You aren't injured?"

"I'm fine," Kaia assured him. Hurt like this, he was worried about her? "I managed to stop him."

"How?" Pinsley asked, and Kaia didn't have an answer for that.

She was grateful in that moment when Xander woke, slumped back against the pillar where Kaia had flung him. She saw the inspector react almost in panic, starting to push her behind him, and reaching out for the spot where his revolver lay on the ground.

"Stay back, Kaia!" he said. "He could still be dangerous."

"He isn't," Kaia insisted. She'd seen the moment when the shadows had fled from him. "It's finished."

"I'm done," Xander assured them from where he lay. "Point a gun at me if you want to, but the shadows are gone. She drove them out."

Kaia could see Pinsley's puzzlement at that. Still, he pushed his way to his feet, moving over to Xander and taking out handcuffs, which he fastened to the other man's wrists.

"You, sir, are under arrest."

*

Inspector Pinsley limped into Great Scotland Yard with one had gripping Xander's arm firmly and the other wrapped around Kaia's shoulders, so that she more or less held him up.

He probably required medical attention, but he had to do this first; he had to bring this to a conclusion. No matter how much his wounds hurt, he forced himself to ignore them as he walked forward to set the sharpened claws of the hand rake down on the duty sergeant's desk.

"Sir?" the sergeant said, obviously not understanding what he was doing there. "Wait, isn't this the girl we're supposed to arrest? And who's this?"

"Sergeant, may I present to you Tabitha Greene's murderer?" Pinsley said, pushing Xander forward. He waited for a moment or two for that to sink in.

The sergeant signaled to a constable. "Go to the superintendent's house. Wake him up and get him here at *once*."

Pinsley motioned the constable over and whispered quickly to him, before letting him go off about his business. He waited there while the constable ran off. The sergeant stared at him, as if not knowing what to do next.

"Sir, we still have orders to arrest the girl," the man said.

"I believe that you should be booking in *this* prisoner, Sergeant," Pinsley pointed out with a look towards Xander. He desperately wanted to find a seat somewhere and rest after everything he'd put his battered body through.

"Um… yes, sir," the sergeant said. "It's just… what actual evidence do we have that-"

"That he committed the crime?" Pinsley said. "Aside from the murder weapon?" He turned to Xander. "Tell him."

"I did this," Xander said. "I went to Bedlam, pretending to see another inmate there. I picked the lock on Tabitha Greene's cell to speak with her. There, my own madness overwhelmed me, and I slew her."

"Is that good enough for you, Sergeant?" Pinsley asked.

"For me?" the sergeant said. "Yes, sir, but I don't know how the superintendent will react to this. I'll log this one in and put him in a cell."

The sergeant wrote Xander's details in the log book, leading him off towards the cells. He was still gone when Pinsley heard the sound of the door opening behind him.

"Pinsley? What do you think you are doing here? And... wait, that's the girl. Have you brought her in?"

Pinsley undid his overcoat before he turned, making sure that Superintendent Hutton would be able to see the blood covering his shirt.

"What madness is this?" the superintendent demanded. "Have you been attacked?"

"Yes," Pinsley said. "By Tabitha Greene's real killer."

"This again?" Hutton said. He marched forward. "Does that mean that you have continued your investigations, in spite of my express instructions otherwise?"

Pinsley knew how dangerous that question would be under other circumstances. He had disobeyed orders to keep investigating. Right then though, he didn't care.

"I've uncovered the truth, Superintendent. Presumably we still care about that in the police?"

Hutton laughed at that. "So you've been off concocting some plot to try to stop a madwoman from being hanged? I don't understand why you've gone to all of this trouble, man. One might almost think that there was something... inappropriate between you and this woman from Bedlam."

Pinsley stared at him. "You really can't understand that an inspector might want the truth?"

"The truth? The *truth* is that you went against your superior's direct orders," Hutton said. "Someone seize that girl. I'm going to enjoy seeing the commissioner's face when you try to explain all of this after you're brought up in front of a disciplinary hearing."

"Oh, he won't have to wait that long, Hutton," a voice from the doorway said.

All of this was worth it, just for the look on the superintendent's face in that moment. The two of them turned to face the newcomer. Even at sixty-two years of age, Sir Richard Mayne was a man of military bearing, and he'd come in full police uniform, with the insignia of his rank on full display. He was clean shaven, with a high forehead and white hair.

"Sir," Superintendent Hutton said, snapping to attention. Even Pinsley made an effort to stand straighter, in spite of the pain he was currently in.

"Inspector," Mayne said. "Please explain to me why constables are dragging me from my bed at this time of night."

"I'm sorry to disturb you, sir," Pinsley said. "But I thought you would want to see this."

"See you exceeding your authority?" Hutton demanded. "You say that you have brought in Tabitha Greene's killer but you have no right to arrest anyone."

"The killer came here with me willingly," Pinsley said. "And has confessed in full."

"And of course, a citizen may make an arrest under the law when they see a crime being committed," Commissioner Mayne said. "As you are fond of pointing out, Superintendent, the police are a civilian force. *Was* a crime being committed, Pinsley?"

"Well, sir," Pinsley said, gesturing to the blood on his shirt. He couldn't keep from enjoying this, at least a little. "The man in question attacked me and inflict these wounds. Does that count?"

"I believe it does," Commissioner Mayne said. He turned to Superintendent Hutton. "Hutton, rather than berating the inspector, I believe you should be thanking him for keeping an innocent woman from being hanged."

"I…" Superintendent Hutton seemed to be struggling for the correct words. "Yes, sir."

"And as part of your gratitude, I think you should drop this nonsense about trying to dismiss Pinsley, don't you?" Commissioner Mayne said.

There was another pause from the superintendent, as he looked from Pinsley to the commissioner and back again.

"Yes, sir," the superintendent said.

"There's the matter of Kaia here, too," Pinsley said. He hadn't forgotten about her. "There were some false allegations of theft against her."

Superintendent Hutton's eyes widened at that. "Is the inspector suggesting that we should ignore crimes now?"

"I'm saying that nothing was actually taken," Pinsley said. "That at this distance in time there is very little actual proof beyond the word of one constable. That if it *does* come to a trial, I will stand up and provide a very thorough recommendation on Kaia's behalf, detailing her role in helping to bring a killer to justice when my own superintendent ignored the facts."

"You wouldn't," Hutton said.

"Based on what I know of Pinsley," Commissioner Mayne said. "I believe that he might. Embarrassing authority is one of the things he was always better at. On the whole, I believe it might be better if we let the matter of the girl drop, don't you?"

This time, Pinsley could practically hear the superintendent grinding his teeth.

"Yes sir," Hutton said.

"And I think you and I should have a talk, in your office."

Pinsley couldn't help feeling a note of triumph as the two men headed off upstairs. It was enough to keep him from almost collapsing until they were both well out of sight.

"Are you all right?" Kaia asked him, as she helped him to a chair.

"I'm better than all right," Pinsley said. "Kaia, you've helped me bring a killer to justice. Without you, an innocent woman might have hanged. I still don't fully understand what you did back there, but I am more grateful than I can express. Ask anything of me, and I swear I will do all I can to make it happen."

He wasn't sure what he expected her to ask of him right then. Probably that she could continue to stay in the vicarage, or for help finding a more permanent life for herself.

Instead, Kaia asked him one thing that Pinsley did *not* expect.

"May I... may I speak with Xander?" she asked.

"That is not safe, Kaia," Pinsley said.

"Please," Kaia begged him, and Pinsley could hear how earnest she was. "I need to know. I have to know."

Pinsley gave in. He, of all people, knew how important family was.

EPILOGUE

Kaia knew the cells by now, but she had never stood on this side of the bars. It didn't do much to take away the sense of oppression. Xander sat in a cell by himself, as if the police were afraid of the danger he would be to other prisoners. He sat on the cold floor, staring back at her through the bars.

The desk sergeant stood beside Kaia, and his stern look said quite clearly that he didn't approve of any of this. Only Pinsley's authority meant that Kaia was here at all.

"Five minutes," the sergeant said, as he stepped away. "And don't get too close to the bars. A man like that can still be dangerous, even locked up."

Kaia knew exactly how dangerous Xander could be, but there was no sign of the shadow in him now, so that he didn't *look* dangerous, he just looked... broken. She waited until she was sure that the sergeant was gone before she spoke. The only reason that she'd waited this long was that she hadn't wanted the inspector to hear. As wedded to logic as he was, he wouldn't understand.

"Tell me more," she said. Xander didn't look at her at first. "*Please* tell me more. You went to Tabitha because she was a shadow-seer? Well, if I'm one too, shouldn't you at least tell me what that means?"

"It means you're in danger," Xander said, looking up at her with haunted eyes.

"From you?" Kaia asked. After all, he'd attacked her once already. She didn't think he could manage it from inside a cell, but even so, she took a small step back from the bars.

Xander shook his head. "Not from me. When I went to Tabitha, the idea was to get her out of there, to free her before..."

"Before what?" Kaia asked.

"Before *they* got to her," Xander said. "They'll come for me now."

"Who are they?" Kaia asked. Even though she'd seen the shadows for herself, some of this still sounded like the ravings of a madman. "What is all this really about, Xander?"

"I didn't want to hurt her," he said, rubbing his hands across his face. "But I was weak. The shadows…"

"I know about the shadows," Kaia said.

Xander laughed then, and there was a brittle edge to that laugh. "No, you don't. You've seen them, but you don't understand what it all means. You weren't brought up with the prophecy ringing in your ears. I felt how powerful you are. With the way the shadows wanted you… it's you, it has to be."

None of this was making any sense to Kaia.

"What has to be me?" she asked.

"Don't be weak like me," Xander said. "You could be the strongest of all of us, but if you're weak, they can take you just the same."

"Who can?" Kaia asked. "The shadows?"

She was getting frustrated. Xander was giving her fragments of this, but not even close to enough.

He nodded. "You have to learn before they get to you. Avoid drunkenness, opium, hatred. They all open ways for the shadows. Focus on the light."

"Is that why you lit the candles?" Kaia asked. She got the feeling that Xander wanted to tell her everything, but that he was struggling to put it all together in his mind. She saw him shuddering there on the floor, huddled in on himself in spite of his size.

"For so long, they hid away in the dark, but people shone lights down into the dark places, opened doors that should not be opened. The shadows poured out. They want a world with no light. I felt it when they were in me."

"They're not a part of you anymore," Kaia said.

"You saved me," Xander agreed. He seemed grateful for a moment, but then fear overtook him again. "But it's too late. They already know. They made me tell them."

"Tell them what?" Kaia asked. "What did you tell them, Xander?"

"I told them about the others, about Paris," the big man said. There were tears in his eyes now. "I betrayed them. I didn't want to…They tortured me. Now they know where the others live. Now they will seek them out. They will kill them. You…you're our last hope. You have to warn them. To stop the attack before it's too late. You have to go….to Paris."

Kaia was speechless. *Paris*. The name evoked some far-off place, a place she had never dreamed of seeing. She had barely even seen her own city of London. She didn't know what to think. Were these the ravings of a drug-ravaged mind?

"Paris??" she repeated, stunned. It seemed like a world away to Kaia. "How can I?"

"The war is starting…. You have to save the others. You have to learn to be what you're meant to be. And, most of all, you have to…"

"What?" Kaia asked, as he started to tail off.

He looked right at her, his haunted eyes piercing her, pleading with her, shining with what Kaia saw instantly was the truth.

"You have to save your sister."

NOW AVAILABLE!

SHADOWSEER: PARIS
(Shadowseer, Book Two)

"This novel succeeds—right from the start…. A superior fantasy…It begins, as it should, with one protagonist's struggles and moves neatly into a wider circle…."
–*Midwest Book Review* (re *Rise of the Dragons*)

"Filled with non-stop action, this novel is sure to keep you on the edge of your seat from cover to cover….Rice is setting up for an amazing series to rival series such as Tamora Pierce's Song of the Lioness, with her strong female protagonist making waves in her world and building the confidence of young women in ours."
–*The Wanderer*, A Literary Journal (re *Rise of the Dragons*)

From #1 bestselling author Morgan Rice, a USA Today bestseller and critically-acclaimed author of the fantasy series *The Sorcerer's Ring* (over 3,000 five-star reviews) and the teen fantasy series *The Vampire Journals* (over 1,500 five-star reviews) comes a groundbreaking new series and genre, where fantasy meets mystery.

SHADOWSEER: PARIS (Book Two) continues the story of Kaia, 17, an orphan coming of age in the Victorian Europe of the 1850s. Kaia yearns to escape her horrific orphanage, to discover who her parents were, and to understand why she can sense shadows when others cannot. When the brilliant Detective Pinsley, 45, takes Kaia under his wing and enlists her help in solving a series of mysterious and bizarre murders sweeping over Europe, the two of them become unlikely partners.

Are they part of a greater war of light versus dark? And is Kaia the only one who can stop it?

Dark fantasy meets mystery in SHADOWSEER, a page-turning, atmospheric thriller packed with authentic period detail, with twists and cliffhangers that will leave you on the edge of your seat. Kaia, a broken hero, will capture your heart as she struggles to claw her way up from the depths, and to solve unsolvable crimes. Fans of books such as *Spellbreaker, The Dresden Files, Mortal Instruments* and *Dr. Jekyl and Mr. Hyde* will find much to love in SHADOWSEER, satisfying fantasy fans who appreciate mystery and suspense, and mystery lovers who want something new, a clean hybrid that will appeal to both adult and young adult readers. Get ready to be transported to another world—and to fall in love with characters you will never forget.

"Morgan Rice proves herself again to be an extremely talented storyteller....This would appeal to a wide range of audiences, including younger fans. It ended with an unexpected cliffhanger that leaves you shocked."
–*The Romance Reviews* (re the paranormal series *Loved*)

"The beginnings of something remarkable are there."
–*San Francisco Book Review* (re the young adult fantasy *A Quest of Heroes*)

SHADOWSEER: MUNICH (Book #3), SHADOWSEER: ROME (Book #4) and SHADOWSEER: ATHENS (Book #5) are also available.

About Morgan Rice

Morgan Rice is the #1 bestselling and USA Today bestselling author of the epic fantasy series THE SORCERER'S RING, comprising seventeen books; of the #1 bestselling series THE VAMPIRE JOURNALS, comprising twelve books; of the #1 bestselling series THE SURVIVAL TRILOGY, a post-apocalyptic thriller comprising three books; of the epic fantasy series KINGS AND SORCERERS, comprising six books; of the epic fantasy series OF CROWNS AND GLORY, comprising eight books; of the epic fantasy series A THRONE FOR SISTERS, comprising eight books; of the new science fiction series THE INVASION CHRONICLES, comprising four books; of the fantasy series OLIVER BLUE AND THE SCHOOL FOR SEERS, comprising four books; of the fantasy series THE WAY OF STEEL, comprising four books; of the fantasy series AGE OF THE SORCERERS, comprising eight books; and if the new fantasy series SHADOWSEER, comprising three books (and counting). Morgan's books are available in audio and print editions, and translations are available in over 25 languages.

Morgan loves to hear from you, so please feel free to visit www.morganricebooks.com to join the email list, receive a free book, receive free giveaways, download the free app, get the latest exclusive news, connect on Facebook and Twitter, and stay in touch!

Made in the USA
Las Vegas, NV
18 October 2021